IN AT THE

In at the Shallow End ... novel. It is set in Ox... author lives, and ... characters – Poppy, ~~Diane~~ and Jenny – who appeared in the Walker paperback *Our Horrible Friend*. Her first novel was *In Between Times* and she has also written two Redwings, *On the Night Watch* and *Kick-Off*, published by Julia MacRae Books.

Hannah Cole read psychology at King's College, Cambridge and then, for five years, taught adults with learning difficulties. She later worked in a nursery school and is now a full-time writer. She has two sons and a daughter.

Some reviews of *In at the Shallow End:*

"This is not only a very good read, with interesting and lively descriptions of the lovely city in which the story is set, but also sometimes a very moving one."
School Librarian

"The story is beautifully written, it has fun and meaning, and it is founded in reality. What more could one ask?"
The Junior Bookshelf

"A great deal of food for thought for older readers."
The Times Educational Supplement

IN AT THE SHALLOW END

HANNAH COLE

WALKER BOOKS
LONDON

First published 1989 by Julia MacRae Books

This edition published 1990 by
Walker Books Ltd
87 Vauxhall Walk, London SE11 5HJ

Printed in Great Britain by Cox and Wyman Ltd, Reading

British Library Cataloguing in Publication Data
Cole, Hannah
In at the shallow end.
I. Title
823'.914 [J]   PZ7
ISBN 0-7445-1477-0

For Claire and Sarah Hull

Chapter

≈ 1 ≈

Dawn and Lisa's father was supposed to be waiting for them at the coach station in Oxford.

"Do you think we will recognise him?" Lisa asked.

"Grown-ups don't change," said Dawn. "Except when they get old. He'll look the same as he used to."

"But I don't even remember what he used to look like," said Lisa. "I wish we had gone to visit him while he was in Australia. He could have sent us the plane tickets. Then we wouldn't have forgotten what he was like."

"It costs a thousand pounds to go to Australia," said Dawn. "But it doesn't matter if we don't recognise him. He will know who we are, because Mum sent him our school photograph."

"He probably won't believe we're us, then," said Lisa. "You had your glasses off, and we were looking all neat in school clothes."

"We look very neat now," said Lisa. Mum had bought them new clothes for the holiday. They normally wore out their old clothes during the holidays, and bought new ones for the start of the next school term, but Mum said she wanted their father to see them looking their best after all these years, so they had all gone into town and spent a fortune.

Dawn looked down at her orange shorts and striped top, and the white trainers that still looked brand new. She shook her head to feel the short hair round her ears and the cool feeling at the back of her neck. Mum had given them both a haircut last night, so that it wouldn't matter so much if they forgot to brush their hair properly while they were in Oxford.

"I suppose we do look different from the photograph. Still, there aren't any other children our age on the coach. He'll know it's us."

They looked out of the window. Cars slid past. There were things to see that could have been interesting if they had been travelling on a country bus, with the chance of getting off at the next stop to explore. But sitting in an air-conditioned coach, travelling at sixty-five miles an hour down the middle lane of the motorway, knowing that the next fresh air they breathed would be in Oxford, there seemed little point in getting interested in the farms that sailed by, even the one with the goats; and the children in the back gardens of the little rows of houses vanished too quickly for Dawn and Lisa to guess what they might have been playing.

"What are you going to call him?" Lisa asked suddenly.

"Who?" said Dawn. She had noticed a broken-down car on the hard shoulder, and was looking out for its driver, who must have gone to phone for a breakdown truck.

Lisa thought for a minute. "Our father."

Dawn laughed. "Not that, anyway. We used to call him Daddy."

"It sounds a bit babyish now, doesn't it?" said Lisa.

"How about Dad?"

"Hmm. It would have been all right if we had grown into it, but it seems strange suddenly to start calling someone Dad."

"I've always thought of him as Jeff," said Dawn. "That's what Mum calls him. And when he wrote to us, he put 'J' at the end, didn't he? 'Love, J'. J for Jeff."

"I suppose so," said Lisa. "But it does sound a bit weird when people call their parents by their first names, doesn't it?"

"You're thinking of those kids across the road," said Dawn. "It only sounds weird for them because their dad is called Edgar."

"I just shan't call him anything," said Lisa.

A very small child tottered up the gangway of the coach, dropping crisps as it went from a big bag that it was holding. Its father came after it, picked it up and took it back to its seat. In a rage, it threw the whole bag on the floor, and then screamed for its lost crisps.

"Do you think he'll let us go out on our own?" Lisa asked.

"What?" Dawn watched the child arching its back

as it sat on its father's lap, and the father growing red with shame at owning such a troublesome child.

"Well, he said he wouldn't be able to amuse us all the time, didn't he? I suppose while he's marking those exam papers we could go out to the park or somewhere, couldn't we? Are there parks in Oxford?"

"I think all towns have parks," said Dawn. "But he might expect us to sit indoors and read while he's working. He is a teacher, after all. He'll probably set us homework to do."

Lisa looked worried.

"Oh, stop thinking about it. I don't know what he's going to be like, do I? Just wait and see."

"Dawn."

"Yes?"

"Are you sure this is the right coach for Oxford?"

"The driver checked our tickets when we got on. He would have told us if we'd been on the wrong one."

They both looked out anxiously for signs to Oxford.

"Dawn, I feel a bit sick. What shall I do if I think I'm going to be sick?"

"Just don't be."

Dawn closed her eyes, to protect herself from any more questions. A few minutes later they were both asleep, Lisa leaning on Dawn's arm.

"Come on, Dawn," a man was saying impatiently.

"Wake up, Lisa. Aren't you getting off?"

"Are we at Oxford?" Dawn asked sleepily. She knew that it must be Oxford, and this must be her father, but she had to say something to wake herself up.

"Of course you are. Come on, the driver's waiting for you. And bring that rubbish, if it's yours."

The rubbish was the comic that Lisa had been reading. Of course, if their father was a teacher he would not approve of comics.

"Our luggage," said Dawn, picking up the comic. "The suitcase. It's in the boot." She picked up her bag and staggered down the gangway between the seats.

"I've got one suitcase with your name on," said her father. "Is that all you brought? I hope you've got enough stuff to last you for a fortnight." He steered Lisa along the gangway and helped her down the steep steps. Their suitcase was waiting on the pavement. It did look small. As soon as they were off the bottom step, the coach doors shut with a loud hiss, the engine roared and the coach sped away.

Dawn had remembered her father as being very tall. He seemed to have shrunk. His hair had turned grey in places, too, and he had shaved off his beard.

"Well?" he said, putting an arm round each girl's shoulder. "What's it like to see your daddy again after all this time?"

They looked awkwardly at each other, half

11

smiling. He stepped back, and looked at them from top to bottom.

"I knew you would be taller, but you do look very grown-up."

Dawn thought that perhaps he did not like the clothes they were wearing. He was wearing new jeans, dark bright-blue with the bottoms properly sewn up, and a check shirt.

"Was the journey all right?"

"Yes, thank you."

"And how's your mother?"

"All right."

"We'd better go straight back and you can sort out your luggage and have something to eat. You hungry?"

Dawn and Lisa nodded. The crisps and chocolate that Mum had given them for the journey seemed a long time ago now, and Lisa was not feeling sick any more.

"We can catch a bus from St Giles. Here, I'll carry the case. What do you think of Oxford? Look, this is one of the colleges. We can have a look round some of them while you are here. Lovely old buildings."

Dawn looked up at the old grey stone building. There was barbed wire at the top of the high stone wall, and a huge gate guarded the entrance.

"It looks like a prison," she said.

Her father laughed, but his face was not smiling. She thought that she had said something wrong. They walked in silence to the bus stop.

Dawn did not know what time it was when she woke the next morning. It was light, but in July that did not mean that it was time to get up. Her watch was on the floor near the bed, but if she moved to reach it, she might wake Lisa, who was sleeping at the other end of the same mattress. It had taken them a while the night before to arrange their legs so that they had enough room. Luckily Lisa curled up in a ball once she was asleep, so Dawn was able to spread out at her end.

Their mattress bed was in a big low room. There were two small windows at floor level, and the sloping ceiling was made of white-painted planks. The floor was varnished wood-coloured planks. There was a round wooden table in the middle of the room which their father had made himself. He had told them about it proudly. There was a record player on the floor, and some big cushions for sitting on, and a strange set of bookshelves made of planks balanced on white-painted bricks. This was their father's living room.

Through the windows, Dawn could see the tops of trees. The room was in the attic of a big house, and the trees were in its garden.

"Dawn!" Lisa whispered. "Are you awake? Is it time to get up?"

Dawn reached out for her watch. "It's only seven," she whispered back. "He may not get up this early. We'd better be quiet."

They slid out from under the blankets and put their clothes on silently.

"Dawn, I need to go to the loo."

"You can't," whispered Dawn. "It's downstairs. You'll wake everybody up."

"I've got to."

"Well, go on then, but be quiet."

"Come with me," Lisa whispered. "I might not be able to find it."

A lot of other people lived downstairs in the big house, and they all shared the bathroom. Their father had shown them where it was last night.

"I might meet one of the downstairs people."

"Well, that's all right," said Dawn. "They won't eat you."

"Please, Dawn."

Dawn got up off the mattress and straightened the pillows, one at each end, and the blankets, in case their father should come in while they were downstairs.

"All right."

The stairs down from the attic were narrow bare wooden steps, closed in with wooden walls on either side and a door at the bottom. It was hard to walk quietly down them, even without shoes on. The steps creaked. At the foot of the stairs there were a lot of doors leading off the landing. All of them were closed.

"That's the bathroom," whispered Dawn. "Go on."

"Are you sure?" asked Lisa. The doors all looked alike. She turned the handle.

"It won't open, Dawn. You try it."

Dawn tried it, and then jumped back when a voice from inside called out, "All right, won't be a minute!"

They looked at each other in horror, and Lisa darted back to the foot of the stairs.

"It's all right," Dawn whispered. "We'll just wait for them to come out."

After a lot of swishing noises, and gurgling as water was let out of the basin, a clean, pink man came out of the bathroom with a towel over his shoulders.

"Sorry," he said. "All yours now." He disappeared through one of the other doors.

Lisa went into the bathroom while Dawn waited for her. A wide staircase with carved banisters led down to the ground floor. There was a nice smell of coffee coming from downstairs, where the main kitchen was. The attic upstairs had its own little kitchen, which Dawn was glad about. It meant that they would not always have to eat with the downstairs people. Her father had said that they sometimes shared meals. The other people only had one room each, but he had the whole attic to himself, with a bedroom, a living room, and the kitchen.

Down here on the landing the doors looked heavy and thick and the ceilings were high. Dawn thought that it should have been a grand house for rich people with lots of servants, but it was very dusty and it looked as though none of it had been painted for hundreds of years. There were no carpets anywhere.

Suddenly footsteps came up the stairs. Somebody wearing shoes, and not taking care to be quiet. It was a woman with very long hair, carrying a mug of coffee and a pile of thick slices of bread and butter.

"Hello," she said. "You Jeff's little girl?" She went into her own room and closed the door.

At last Lisa came out of the bathroom and they went back upstairs to the attic.

"Come and look out of the window," said Lisa. She had pulled a big cushion over, to look out in comfort.

"Don't sit so close to the glass," said Dawn. "If you fell through you'd go all the way down to the garden. You'd be dead."

She was tidying their pyjamas into the suitcase, which was going to be their wardrobe while they were staying with their father. He kept all his own clothes in cardboard boxes in his bedroom. There were no cupboards or chests of drawers.

"I couldn't fall through," said Lisa. "Come and look. You can see the whole garden from up here."

"Ssh," hissed Dawn. "You'll wake him up. If he's anything like Mum, he'll want a good lie-in when he's got the chance."

"He's not asleep," said Lisa. "He's down there."

Dawn bent down to look through the window. Their father was down in the garden. He was wearing a tracksuit, and he came jogging across the lawn towards the house.

"We were trying to be so quiet," said Dawn indignantly, in her usual voice, "and he was outside all the time!"

"I wonder if he goes out running every morning?" said Lisa. "I could go with him. I like running."

They heard their father's footsteps on the creaky wooden staircase, and he came bouncing into the living room.

"Up at last?" he said, and bent to touch his toes a few times. "Sleep all right?"

"Yes, thank you."

"Let's get you some breakfast." He went through to the kitchen and proudly showed them a packet of cornflakes.

"I got some cereal in for you. I don't eat it myself."

He put the kettle on and found three mugs.

"This is the mug you gave me for my birthday, Dawn, do you remember? Oh, it must have been four or five years ago now."

Dawn looked at the mug. It had a picture of a yellow cat on roller skates on the side. She felt that she had never seen it before in her life, but she smiled and nodded. The mug was chipped. Their father didn't seem to have any nice things.

"Are you going to be working all day today?" Lisa asked.

"No," said her father. "I'm taking the morning off. I thought we could walk down into town. There's a tower that you're allowed to climb up, and a friend of mine said that he was taking his kids up there this morning. We might meet them."

Dawn wondered why they should want to climb up a tower. Lisa thought it was a bit hot for walking all the way into town. It had seemed a long way in the bus yesterday. They wondered what the friend's children would be like.

"That would be nice," said Dawn.

Chapter

≈ 3 ≈

Instead of walking into town on the hard pavements of the long road that the bus had come along, they walked down behind the house. The road led to a wide green field. A few horses were grazing there. It seemed a strange place to find in the middle of a city.

"Are we in the country?" Lisa asked. "I thought Oxford was a big city?"

"Well, I live right on the edge of Oxford," said her father. "But this meadow goes all the way into town. It's where I come to run every morning. It's an interesting place. There are circular marks in the grass where there used to be huts in the Bronze Age."

"I can't see any circles," said Lisa. They looked across the rough grass. On the far side of the green expanse Dawn could see something gliding along. It seemed to be low down on the ground, and moving far too steadily to be an animal.

"No, no, you wouldn't be able to see them from here. But from an aeroplane they are clearly visible. I've got some aerial photographs at home. I'll show you when we get back. You can see rectangles as well, which show that there were cattle enclosures here centuries ago. In fact the meadow has been used for grazing animals for as long as anyone can tell."

Lisa sighed. Dawn remembered that her father was a teacher.

They were crossing the meadow. At the far edge of the grass were trees, and beyond them Dawn could see a few towers and a dome. Another of the strange low flat things moved along through the grass over to their right. Dawn stared at it, trying to make sense of it. She took off her glasses and gave them a polish with the edge of her T-shirt, but the thing still looked much the same. It had square markings on its side. Its eyes glinted. Dawn wondered whether her father had noticed. Perhaps these things were part of what made the meadow so interesting.

"Look!" said Lisa. "A boat! You didn't say there was a river, Daddy! Can we go over there and look at it?"

Of course the moving things were boats! It was obvious. The glinting eyes were the front windows. They must be moving along low down between the grassy banks of the river, and from here you could only see the top half of them. Here came another one. Dawn was glad that she had not asked her father what they were.

Lisa led them closer to the river, which seemed to be winding towards the spiky roofs of Oxford. Dawn followed, watching out for horses. Most of them were busy munching and ignored anything that was not grass.

"Do you know what river this is?" her father asked.

"No." How could she know.

"It's the Thames, the same river that flows under London Bridge. Hard to believe, isn't it?"

The river was narrow, only about as wide as an ordinary street. In one place the grassy bank had worn away and some black and white cows were standing in wet mud at the edge of the water. Lisa ran down to join them.

"You'll get muddy," her father warned.

Another boat came by, not mysterious at all. It was gaily painted in red and green and two men lay sunbathing on its roof while a third steered. Lisa jumped back to escape the waves that it made.

On the opposite bank a woman sat reading a newspaper. Nearby, on a tiny patch of beach at the edge of the river, her little girl squatted in the muddy sand trying to make castles. She let the wash from the boat splash over her bare feet and wet the bottoms of her trousers.

"Can we paddle?" Lisa asked.

"Perhaps another time. Let's hurry on into town, or we'll miss Dave."

They passed a crowd of boats tied up at the edge of the water. Dawn read some of their names: *Queen of the Isis*, *Shawford Lily*.

Then they crossed a bridge, and were on a proper

21

path that led alongside the river.

"My legs are tired, Daddy," said Lisa. Dawn was surprised. She would not have dared complain herself, even if their father had made them walk twenty miles. And she still did not think of him as Daddy, or Dad.

"Not much further now," he said briskly. "This path will take us all the way into Oxford."

Suddenly they were among buildings again and the river disappeared under a road. Oxford looked like any other town. There were even the same shops as the ones that Dawn and Lisa were used to at home. Children cried in their push-chairs and adults walked too fast or too slow along the crowded pavements, always in the wrong direction. Lisa held her father's hand and Dawn followed them, trying to keep close behind.

"Is that the tower?" Lisa asked.

"No, that belongs to one of the colleges. I don't think you are allowed up that one. Here's the one we are going up," said her father.

At the foot of the tower, the heavy wooden door was open and a sign gave the times that the tower was open to the public, and the cost of admission.

Their father had noticed the sign as well. "Fifty pence!" he said, screwing up his face as though he had bitten something sour. "I didn't realise it was going to be that expensive!"

"Oh, that doesn't matter," said Lisa. "Mum gave us some money for the holiday, didn't she, Dawn?

We can pay if you can't afford it, Daddy."

"Don't be silly," said her father, embarrassed. "Of course I can afford it. I just think it's rather expensive, that's all."

They followed him inside. He paid for them all and started up the spiral staircase which wound round behind a stone wall and disappeared. The steps were triangular, with a wide part near the outside wall, but tapering to a point at the inside of the curve. They walked up on the wide parts, holding on to a rail on the wall, until they met some people coming down. Then they had to squeeze over to the narrow side and stand very still while the people went past. A camera hanging round one of the people's necks swung out and hit Dawn on the head.

The spiral staircase led to a high room with a wooden floor. Dawn began to wish that they had not come. From this room a black metal staircase led up through a hole in the roof. A woman was leading a nervous little boy down it, encouraging him at the same time as trying to prevent a toddler from walking through the wide bars at the side of the stairs. Underfoot, the steps were like lace, with holes in them making patterns of leaves and flowers. The little boy did not like being able to see down through them to the floor below.

When the woman and children were down, Lisa started off up towards the ceiling. Dawn followed, firmly looking neither up nor down, but at the rail where her hand was holding on. Her father was not even holding on, but walking briskly up as though he were on the solid stairs at home.

At the top of the iron staircase was another stone one. Dawn preferred this sort, because you couldn't see very far in any direction, and she didn't have to think about falling.

Another group of people came down and she had to wait for them to pass, and then she saw that Lisa and their father were already out in the sunlight. She climbed up to meet them, blinked, and found that the tower was a good deal higher than it had seemed from the ground.

"It's Jeff!" someone shouted.

"Here at last!"

"We've been waiting for ages!"

"We thought you were never coming, Jeff," a man said. "So these are your girls, are they?"

"Yes, this is Lisa, and this is Dawn."

"Hello," said the man. He was holding on to one of the girls by her pony-tail as she peered over the low stone wall. "I'm Dave. This one that I've got tethered is Jennifer, and those two over there are Poppy and Diane."

There were some other children at the top of the tower, but it seemed that only these three belonged to Dave.

"I don't mind if you call me Jenny," said the one called Jennifer. "Let go, Dad. I want to walk about."

"No chance," said her dad. "Not after you tried to

fly just then."

"I was only looking over to see whether there were any gargoyles."

"What are gargoyles?" Lisa asked.

Jenny made an awful face, rolling her eyes and pulling the sides of her mouth out with her thumbs. "Like that," she said, "only made of stone, and some of them have wings and horns and tusks. Sometimes water comes gushing out of their mouths. If you walk along there you see loads of them on the colleges."

She pointed down to one of the roads that led away from the tower. Buses were following each other slowly along it. Lisa went to lean over the edge next to Jenny. Dawn looked at Dave's children. All three girls looked about the same size, but none of them seemed to be twins. Perhaps Diane was a bit older than the others. Dawn smiled slightly at them and then went to look over the parapet.

Far below people went in and out of shops, crossed the road just in front of a bus, tripped over each other's bags. Dawn felt that her head was no longer sure which way up it was meant to be. She stopped looking straight down at what was just below her, and walked round, inspecting the roofs of the nearby shops. When she looked at the green hills in the distance she could almost forget that she was high up.

Her father was telling his friend Dave what the different domes and spires were. They were arguing about one of them. Dave let go of Jenny's hair and Dawn watched anxiously as she leant over the edge. Lisa and the girl called Poppy leant near her. They were making gargoyle faces and pretending to gush water on to the people standing below. Their fathers were in charge, so Dawn could not tell them not to lean over, but she felt that by staring at them she could keep their feet safely on the firm roof. Each time one of them leaned further, she felt a tight grip in her stomach. When Lisa took one foot off the ground to scratch her other leg with it, Dawn let out a quiet "Oh!", but Lisa just put her foot down again without noticing.

"Do you like it?" asked Dave. "Quite a view, isn't it?"

"Yes, it's nice," said Dawn, wishing they were down again. She might have enjoyed the tower on her own, but she felt quite exhausted by the effort of keeping her eyes fixed on Lisa.

"What are you planning to do while you are here?" Dave asked.

"Oh, I think I'll just look at the view," said Dawn, a little puzzled. "I like all the spires and things."

"I mean while you are in Oxford," said Dave. "All the rest of the holidays."

Dawn felt silly. "Oh, I don't know. Play in the garden, I suppose, or watch telly, or go to the park. Things like that."

Her father was watching her, and she realised that he wanted her to make a good impression on his friend Dave.

"I'll probably read quite a lot, too," she added. "And play my recorder. And my mum got me a new sketch-book so that I can draw some of the old buildings to show her."

She looked at her father. He seemed satisfied.

"Oh, Jeff," said Dave. "Are you busy tomorrow morning? Rosa's taking the kids over to her mother's, and I wondered if you fancied a game of squash at the Ferry Centre."

"I would," said Jeff. "But what about Dawn and Lisa? It wouldn't be much fun for them, just watching."

"They could have a swim while we play," said Dave. "I've done that with our lot sometimes. The pool is right next to the squash courts, you know. We could have a swim ourselves, after we've played."

"All right," said Jeff. "Ten o'clock? Are you going to book the court?"

Nobody had asked Dawn or Lisa what they thought of the plan. Dawn worried about it as they followed Dave down the tower. The stairs seemed steeper going this way, and the backs of Dawn's legs ached as they took her down and down. The metal staircase was awful. Dawn tried not to watch Lisa who was hurrying ahead. It would be so easy to trip here, and it was such a long way to fall.

At last they were down, and stepped back out into the sunlight. Looking up, the tower had shrunk back to its normal size. The other people up at the top didn't look so very far away.

"Can Lisa come round to our house?" Poppy asked Dave.

No-one asked if Dawn could come too.

"Not today," said Dave. "Jeff will want to see her today, it's their first day. We'll ask them over another time. And I'll see you tomorrow at ten, Jeff. I'll ring if I can't book the court, otherwise assume it's all right. 'Bye!"

Dave and the three girls disappeared.

Dawn had been waiting to say something to her father. "I haven't got a swimming costume," she said. "Neither of us has."

"What?" said her father, as though he could not believe it. "Did you forget to bring them?"

"No," said Lisa. "We haven't got any. Why, are we going swimming?"

Their father sighed. "I've just fixed up for you two to go swimming tomorrow while Dave and I have a game of squash. Why couldn't you have mentioned it earlier, Dawn? We could have asked Dave's girls to lend you their things. Oh, this is a nuisance."

"I suppose we could watch you playing squash," said Dawn.

"Oh, no!" said Lisa. "That's boring!"

"We'll just have to buy you a costume each. You're sure to need them while you are staying here. Look, they'll probably have some in this shop."

It was a large department store. Jeff took a twenty pound note from a wallet in his jacket pocket. Dawn wondered why he had made such a fuss about paying fifty pence to go up the tower.

"Here you are," he said, handing her the note.

She took it uncertainly.

"Well, go on. Go and find yourselves a couple of swimming costumes. Not too expensive."

Dawn had never bought any clothes on her own. Usually Mum bought them for her, and sometimes she went with Mum. But Jeff was leaning against a pillar outside the shop and obviously did not mean to come in with them.

Dawn looked at him, hoping that he would change his mind and come in to help, but he was watching a young man who was playing a violin on the pavement and collecting money in the open case.

"Come on," said Dawn to Lisa. They went into the shop.

"Can I choose mine?" Lisa asked.

"We'll have to find out where they are first of all," said Dawn. They found a board on the wall which said *Children's Wear, upper floor*.

"Let's go up the escalator," said Lisa. It took them slowly up.

"They should make spiral escalators for towers," Lisa said. "Those stairs were awful. My legs are still aching."

"There wouldn't be room for a down escalator,"

said Dawn. "Not as well as an up one."

"You could have a pole down the middle," said Lisa. "For sliding down, like they have in fire stations. Look, there's the children's clothes."

There were dresses, socks, shirts, jackets, everything except swimming costumes. Eventually Dawn had to ask one of the shop assistants, who was very busy arranging plastic leaves above a display of handbags.

"Swimwear?" she said, raising her eyebrows very high indeed. "Oh, that would be downstairs."

So they went down again and eventually found swimming costumes arranged round a cardboard seaside scene.

"They're all horrible," said Lisa. "I want a yellow bikini."

"You'll have to choose one of these," said Dawn. "I'm not taking you to another shop. He's waiting for us."

Lisa turned over each of the swimming costumes, as though they might look different on the other side.

"All right," she said eventually. "I'll have one like this." It was blue and yellow stripes. "Oxford United football team colours."

"How do you know?" asked Dawn.

"Poppy told me. That's why the buses are blue and yellow."

Dawn looked at the labels on the striped costumes. "There's only age four to five or ten to eleven," she said. "None of them are your size."

"There must be one," said Lisa, looking at all the labels again. "It's the only sort I like."

Dawn was looking on the other stands to find a costume for herself.

"Oh, look, here's one of the blue and yellow ones that's got on to the wrong rack. This one is your size."

Lisa grabbed it. "Let's go and pay for it quick, before anyone else decides they want it."

"All right," said Dawn. "Just wait while I find one for me."

"Dawn! Lisa! Haven't you got them yet?" Their father had come into the shop and was pushing his way through the stands, making the coat-hangers swing.

"Nearly," said Dawn.

There were some plain black costumes with one multi-coloured stripe across the front. The one that was supposed to be right for Dawn's age looked far too small, just a scrap of material with straps. She picked the next size up.

"All right," she said. "We've each got one. I'd better go and pay."

Her father checked the price tags and sniffed. "I hope you're going to enjoy the swimming, at this price," he said.

Chapter

≈ 4 ≈

"All right then, girls? I'll join you in the pool later on."

Dawn thought how smart her father looked. He was wearing white shorts and a white short-sleeved shirt, and very clean white socks. It was strange that he managed to have clothes that looked so smooth and clean when he just kept them all in cardboard boxes. Dawn and Lisa's clothes were already beginning to look rumpled after two days in the suitcase.

Dave was swinging his racket, impatient to start playing.

"All right," said Dawn. "See you later."

She pushed open the door marked *Female Changing Room* and Lisa followed her in. It was a large room with a tiled floor. Round the edges were low benches, and there were pegs on the wall like a school cloakroom.

"Where are the places for getting changed in?" Lisa asked.

"Here, I think," said Dawn.

A very large old woman was peeling off a big blue swimming costume, and two small children were running about with no clothes on. Their mother chased them with a towel.

"In front of everybody?" said Lisa. "I'm not."

"We'll have to," said Dawn. "He expects us to get in the pool, and he's coming to meet us there after he's played squash. There isn't anywhere else to change. Here, I'll hold your towel up and you can undress behind it."

Lisa agreed to that, and slowly undressed, while Dawn's arms grew tired from holding the towel up to hide her.

"Right," said Lisa, when all her clothes were off. "I'll hold it up for you now."

"It's all right," said Dawn. "I don't mind."

She changed quickly into her swimming costume. It was a little bit loose, but perhaps the water would shrink it. It was annoying that Lisa was not bothering to hide now. Dawn's arms had got tired for nothing.

They left their clothes in neat little heaps on the bench and walked through to the pool. They had to walk through a shallow foot-bath of cold water. It did not look very clean, and Dawn managed to get across in only two steps. There were two pools, blue and sparkling. In the larger one adults were swimming up and down in straight lines. In the small one some toddlers in orange arm-bands were bobbing about, and larger children were jumping and splashing and chasing. There was a loud noise as the splashes and shouts echoed in the huge bare building.

"You should have taken your glasses off," said

Lisa. "Nobody else is wearing them."

"I can't take them off," said Dawn. "I wouldn't be able to see."

"Let's get in, anyway," said Lisa, heading for the larger pool, and pulling Dawn after her.

A man in bathing trunks, who was sitting on a chair at the top of a ladder, leaned down towards them.

"It's lengths only in the deep pool," he said.

"Grown-ups only?" asked Lisa.

"No, lengths. You have to swim up and down. No splashing around."

"Oh. We'd better go in the little pool, then."

Lisa strode down the shallow steps into the water, then sank down until it came up to her chin. "Look, I'm sitting on the bottom! It's really shallow here. Come on, Dawn, it's lovely."

Dawn stood on the top step and felt the warm water round her ankles. On the next step, it was half-way to her knees. Someone dashed past and splashed her. A baby was swimming nearby, kicking its legs happily. Dawn walked down to the bottom step and sat near Lisa with her head above the water.

"It's like a giant bath, isn't it?" said Lisa. She let her legs float to the surface in front of her, just steadying herself by keeping her hands on the bottom of the pool.

"I wonder how long they'll be playing squash?" Dawn said. "I suppose either half an hour or an hour. What are we supposed to do all that time?"

"Play," said Lisa. She bounced up and down and water splashed on to the lenses of Dawn's glasses. Everything blurred. She wiped them as well as she could with her wet fingers.

Lisa splashed her way to the far end of the little pool. It was not deep even there and she could stand in the water easily. Dawn stayed in the shallow end and watched the other swimmers. A grandmother with a flowery plastic swimming cap followed her tiny granddaughter as she bobbed around in the water in a rubber ring.

"Stop splashing!"

"No!"

"Don't shout!"

Splash!

Dawn liked the little girl, who did not seem afraid of the water or of her scolding grandmother. It looked as though the grandmother was half admiring her boldness, too, and was only pretending to be angry.

"Come on, Dawn!" called Lisa. "Come and swim in the deep water. Look, I can swim half-way across!"

She launched herself and kicked wildly, grasping at the water with her hands. Dawn saw her sink lower and lower until at last she stood up, spluttering and shaking the water from her hair. Then she looked round to judge how far she had swum.

"Two metres," she said. "Or do you think it was

three?''

"Two," said Dawn. "It's very good. But I think you would have to breathe if you were going to swim much further."

"I can only swim under water so far," said Lisa. "You try it."

Dawn lowered herself in the water and tried carefully lifting up one foot behind her. She felt unsteady and quickly put it down again.

By the time their father joined them in the pool, she had been sitting on the steps in the shallow end for what felt like hours. She did not recognise him at first. He had just had a shower and his hair was stuck flat down on his head. He was wearing bright flowered swimming shorts.

"What on earth have you got your glasses on for?" he asked. "You haven't even got your hair wet!"

He scooped up a handful of water and splashed her head. "Come on, let's go in the real pool. Lengths-only should have finished by now, and Dave came through ages ago. He's probably swum half a mile already. Where's your sister?"

Lisa came bouncing through the water towards them.

"Come on," said her father. "We're going in the real pool."

"Great," said Lisa. "How deep is it?"

"Not very, not at this end. I should think you could stand in it."

To Dawn's horror, Lisa ran across to the large pool and stepped straight in off the side. Dawn hurried over to see if she came up again. Yes, there she was, blowing out water and shaking her head, but still smiling. Dawn felt her swimming costume hanging loosely round the top of her legs. She looked down and saw that it had stretched. It looked about five sizes too large.

"Come on," said her father, and taking Dawn by the hand he jumped off the edge into the deep water. Dawn was pulled in after him. Her feet touched the bottom, but then the water swirling round her made her lose her balance. Luckily Dave was nearby. He had just come back like a high-speed windmill from the deep end. He pulled Dawn to her feet and handed her her glasses, which had fallen off.

"You can't swim with these on," he said.

"I only want to watch," said Dawn. She made for the side and held on firmly. She felt as though her head, ears, eyes, nose and mouth were all full of water. She had been frightened, and she was angry with her father for scaring her.

"Good grief," he said. "Can't you swim?"

"No," said Lisa. "Neither of us can. But watch me, I've nearly learnt how to do it."

Lisa did not seem to mind the swirling shapeless water all round her. To Dawn it smelt disgusting, full of chemicals. She thought of it in her mouth and it made her feel sick.

"Well, if you can't swim, I suppose we'd better go back to the baby pool," said their father scornfully. "It never occurred to me that at your age you wouldn't know how to swim. It's about time you learnt."

"They run swimming classes here during the holidays," said Dave. "That's how Poppy learnt to swim a couple of years ago. She's starting another course of lessons next week, every morning for five days. She loves it."

"Maybe I should book these two in for some lessons," said Jeff. "I mean it's ridiculous, children as big as these not able to swim. Anyway, we'll leave you to your serious swimming, Dave. We'd better go and paddle in the baby pool."

"See you, then," said Dave.

He shot away from them up the bath, heading for the deep end with his strong arms pulling him through the water.

Jeff hoisted himself out on to the edge of the pool and watched critically as Dawn felt her way to the ladder in the corner, and climbed out. She held her swimming costume up so that it was not hanging down too ridiculously.

"Let's see what you can do, then," he said to Lisa when they were in the shallow pool again. Lisa jumped and dived and swam nearly two and a half metres.

"I'll hold your glasses," he said to Dawn. "You have a go."

But Dawn had had enough water for one day and was glad when they got out and went to get changed. Jeff went to the men's changing room.

"I'll meet you outside the main entrance," he said. "Don't take too long."

Lisa wanted a shower, so Dawn left her enjoying the warm water gushing over her and went on to the changing room to find her towel. The bench where they had left their clothes was empty. Their shoes, which they had left neatly under the bench, had disappeared. Dawn ran back to the showers.

"Lisa! Our clothes have gone! Someone's taken them!"

"Who would want to take our clothes?" said Lisa. "You must have looked in the wrong place."

"I haven't! Besides, they aren't anywhere else either. Come and help look."

"I'll come in a minute," said Lisa. She pressed the button for the shower to switch on again, and turned her face up so that the water fell directly on to it. "It's so warm. Why don't you have a shower, Dawn?"

"Oh, do come," said Dawn. "What are we going to do if everything has been stolen? We can't go home like this! This swimming costume doesn't even fit me, it's like an elephant skin. I'm glad I kept my glasses on, anyway."

Lisa left the warm shower at last and came to look round the changing room. There were heaps of clothes and towels where people were changing, but their little piles were nowhere to be seen.

"I hate this place," said Dawn violently. "It stinks, and the floor isn't even clean."

Lisa looked bewildered, and wandered round the room looking at the different heaps of clothes. All of them belonged to people who were dressing or undressing.

"Where are the clothes that belong to all the other people who are in the pool at the moment?" she said. "They must all have been stolen as well. There aren't any clothes lying around at all."

"Perhaps there aren't any other girls swimming at the moment," said Dawn. "The boys would have left their clothes in the other changing room."

"No," said Lisa, "there definitely were some girls, and those women with the babies as well. I expect one of them will get out in a minute and notice that their clothes are gone. If we wait, someone will call the police and perhaps the swimming pool people will lend us some spare clothes or something."

They stood, wet and cold, and waited. A woman with a little girl came from the pool, took a key from nowhere and unlocked a metal locker on the wall. Inside were some towels and clothes.

"Look," said Dawn. "She had her things in one of those cupboards. Perhaps everyone else put their things in a cupboard, and our clothes were stolen because they weren't put away."

"Go and get the woman who sells the tickets," said Lisa. "We can't stay here for ever."

"You go," said Dawn.

"You're the eldest," said Lisa, and she sat down on a bench.

Dawn opened the door leading to the corridor. People in white clothes walked past, going to the squash courts. She felt very silly in her baggy swimming costume. Holding a handful of it up in front of her, she walked along the corridor making wet footprints on the carpet.

"Dawn!" It was her father. He had come back, tired of waiting outside. "What have you been doing? Hurry up and get dressed! Get back into that changing room! You can't walk about here like that!"

"Our clothes have gone," said Dawn. "Someone has stolen them."

Without another word, her father took her by the arm and dragged her along to the ticket kiosk. Pushing in front of the queue of people waiting to pay for a swim or a game of squash, he said to the woman inside, "My daughter can't find her clothes, and I can't go into the women's changing room to help her look for them. Could you go in and sort it out, please?"

The woman looked at Dawn, who was shivering and feeling that the whole queue was staring at her in her too-large swimming costume.

"Sandra!" she called. Someone else came out from a back room. "Sandra, didn't you say you put away some children's clothes?"

"Yes," said Sandra. "These are the keys. We put

any loose clothes into lockers," she explained, and pointed to a blackboard leaning against the kiosk. Scrawled on it in chalk was this message: *There has been a spate of thefts from the changing rooms. Please use lockers. Any clothes left on benches will be put in lockers, and a charge of 10p made.*

Sandra handed over the keys, and Dawn hurried with them back to the changing rooms. Her father stayed behind to pay the twenty pence. When they joined him five minutes later he told them grimly, "I've booked you in for swimming classes starting next Monday. Nine-thirty every morning for a week." He had meant it to sound like a treat, but the cost of the lessons, and the delay with the lost clothes, had annoyed him. Besides, he was not really looking forward to bringing the children down to the swimming pool every morning.

"It's about time you knew how to look after your own things, and it's high time you learnt to swim."

The night before the first lesson, Jeff said, "Your swimsuit looked awful, Dawn. Why didn't you buy the right size?"

"It stretched," said Dawn. "It was all right until it got wet."

"You had better sew it up, then," said Jeff. "See if you can get it looking a bit more reasonable. I've got a needle and thread somewhere."

He went into his room and fetched a needle, already threaded with blue thread, from one of the cardboard boxes.

"That isn't the right colour," said Lisa. "Dawn's swimming costume is black."

"I only have blue cotton," said Jeff. "I find it matches everything."

Dawn took the needle and wondered what to do with it.

"Just shorten the straps," said Jeff. "Fold a bit over and sew it down."

Dawn folded one of the straps and poked the needle through the doubled cloth. It pulled straight through the other side. Jeff watched and shook his head.

"Don't tell me that your mother hasn't even

taught you how to sew," he said.

"Mum told us not to learn," said Lisa. "We did raffia at school instead. Mum says that if a woman knows how to sew or cook, men will be asking her to sew on their buttons for them and cook their dinners all her life. She says it's easier to say 'No, I can't' than 'No, I won't'."

Jeff took the swimming costume in silence and pricked his finger on the needle. With his lips tight shut he stitched away until both straps were shortened by several inches.

"Try it on," he ordered.

The body of the swimming costume was still a bit large, but it did not sag down any more because the short straps held it well up.

"Thanks," said Dawn, and got dressed again. She had been wondering when Jeff was going to start preparing the tea, but after Lisa saying that they could not cook and did not mean to learn, it was a little awkward. Perhaps he would think it was about time they learnt, and make them cook the tea.

"I'm starving," said Lisa.

"We're eating downstairs tonight," said Jeff. "Gordon will give us a shout when it's ready."

"Are we having tea with all the downstairs people?" Dawn asked.

"Not all of them," said Jeff. "Simon and Mary are away for the weekend, and Philip seems to be on a diet. But I expect the rest will be there."

They had met most of the downstairs people, but

only very briefly. The only television in the house was down in the big shared living room, and on the first evening Jeff had taken Dawn and Lisa down to watch a programme. But someone was waiting all the time to change channels, so they had soon come upstairs again. Until now, Jeff had made all their meals up in the attic kitchen. There was no oven up here, just two gas rings and a grill. They had food out of tins, and sausages, and cheese on toast.

Everyone was very kind at tea-time. Gordon had cooked a huge saucepanful of spaghetti bolognese and did not seem to mind at all when Lisa said she only wanted spaghetti and no bolognese.

"So what do you think of Oxford?" Sarah asked. She was the woman with long hair who had clattered upstairs with a pile of bread and butter on the first morning.

"It's very nice," said Dawn politely.

"More spaghetti, anyone?" Gordon asked hopefully.

"What are your plans for next week?" Sarah asked Dawn. "I suppose Jeff will be working hard at marking his exam papers. How are you and Lisa going to keep busy?"

"We're going to swimming lessons every day," said Dawn. She had been able to think of nothing else since Jeff had announced that he had booked them in for the classes.

"Oh, that's great!" said Sarah. "At the Ferry Centre? It's a lovely pool, isn't it? Are you good at swimming, then?''

''Not very,'' Dawn mumbled.

''Neither of them can swim a stroke!'' Jeff announced. ''At their age! I thought I had better do something about it.''

A pale man at the end of the table, who had been reading while the meal went on, with his book tucked under the edge of his plate to stop the pages flipping over, looked up. ''I can't swim,'' he said. ''And I manage all right.'' He went back to his book.

Dawn felt very grateful to him.

''You'll love it when you can swim,'' said Sarah. ''Gordon goes swimming every morning before breakfast, don't you?''

Gordon nodded. ''I prefer swimming in the sea,'' he said. ''It's a bit dull in these antiseptic swimming pools with no waves.''

''And no dangerous currents dragging you out to sea, and no poisonous jellyfish, or rocks hiding under the surface, or pollution from sewage outlets,'' said Sarah, teasing him.

Dawn was glad that they were a long way from the sea.

Chapter

≈ 6 ≈

Jeff brought his brief-case to the sports centre.

"I'll sit at one of those tables in the spectators' area," he said. "I can see the pool from there, and get on with my marking at the same time."

He pushed open the door into the spectators' area, and Dawn could see the large glass windows which overlooked the two swimming pools. There were several plastic-topped tables with empty paper cups scattered on them.

Jeff turned back to speak to the girls again. "Remember to use a locker this time," he said. "You've got the money, haven't you? And take your glasses off, Dawn." Then he added, "Have fun," and disappeared through the door.

Lisa hurried down the corridor to the changing room. Dawn walked slowly, wishing that she could stretch out the few minutes left before the lesson was due to begin. In the changing room they met Poppy. They hardly recognised her because she was wearing a tight red rubber swimming hat and she looked quite different from when they had met her at the top of the tower.

"Hello," she said. "You'd better get changed quickly. It's nearly time to start."

This time Lisa did not bother to hide behind a towel, and they were soon both ready. Dawn tucked her glasses into one of her shoes before she locked her things into one of the metal lockers on the wall.

"Come on," said Poppy, leading the way through the foot-bath.

A crowd of other children were waiting for the lesson to begin. To Dawn they were a blur of bright colours in their different swimming costumes and trunks. Without her glasses nothing was properly in focus. The two pools looked strange. She could not see what was wrong with them, but for some reason they did not seem to have water in them. Dawn screwed up her eyes and blinked a few times, but still the large blue rectangle and the small one looked quite unlike deep pools full of water.

"There's Daddy," Lisa whispered. "Just by the window. Do you see him?"

"Of course I can't," said Dawn impatiently. She felt very uncomfortable when she could not see properly and it made her cross.

"He's not watching us," Lisa went on. "He's working already. It looks as though he's got his papers spread out on a big sheet of newspaper. Why would he do that, I wonder?"

"I expect the table was sticky," said Dawn. "From people's drinks. He wouldn't want to get his papers dirty."

"Drinks?" said Lisa. "Can you get drinks here? I wonder if he'll get us one after the swimming lesson?"

"Come on," said Poppy. "You have to stand against the wall until the teacher has checked you off on the list."

They followed Poppy to a space by the wall, along by the big pool. Some very small children were standing against the wall near the little pool. Dawn thought that it was very lucky that they had Poppy to tell them what to do, especially when someone in a T-shirt and shorts came and shouted, "Against the wall!" at some children who were too near the water's edge.

Dawn thought of people lined up against a wall to be shot. She watched Poppy to check that there was nothing else they should be doing. The other children in this group seemed about the same age as her. She thought that if her mother could have watched through the glass windows where Jeff was sitting, she would have said, "How nice that you are meeting other children and making friends." But of course it was impossible to make friends when there was the swimming lesson to worry about.

A man in a tracksuit came over and the children quietened down. He began to read names off a list and the children put up their hands to show that they were there. The man knew some of the children who had been in his class before. He recognised Poppy, whose name was near the top of the list. Dawn and Lisa waited for their names to be read out.

"Right," the man said. "Into the pool."

The children dashed to the edge of the pool and slid or jumped into the blue water, and Dawn realised what it was about the pools that had looked so strange before. When no-one was in the water the surface had been perfectly smooth, unlike any water that she had ever seen before, except perhaps in a bath. As soon as the first toe broke the glassy surface, ripples spread out over it and the whole pool looked like water again. Dawn decided that to-morrow she would look at it with her glasses on.

Poppy had not jumped in with the other children. She was watching the man. Dawn realised that he had finished reading his list, and her name and Lisa's were not on it. The man looked at them.

"You can't be in my group," he said. "Try over there."

He pointed to the little pool. Poppy gave them a last encouraging smile and jumped into the water to join the rest of her class. Lisa led the way to the small pool, where tiny children were standing in a group round their teacher. The children looked up at the two newcomers. Dawn imagined that they would expect her, by far the oldest among them, to be the star of the class. She felt ashamed.

"Dawn and Lisa?" the teacher said. "Come along, we've been waiting for you. Are you complete beginners, or can you swim a little?"

"I can swim two metres," said Lisa.

"Never mind," said the teacher. "Better late than

never. Let's see. We normally start children in the shallow end of the little pool, but as you are both rather bigger than normal perhaps you had better come in the deep end. Follow me."

"I'm not bigger than normal," Lisa whispered to Dawn. "I'm always this size." But Dawn did not feel like laughing.

The teacher led half of the small children to the deep end of the little pool, and Dawn and Lisa followed them. The other children, who could not swim at all, stayed at the shallow end where another teacher encouraged them to put their feet in the water.

"Let's see you all jump into the water," said the teacher. Most of the children jumped. Dawn knew that she could not jump. She felt Lisa beside her, wanting to jump but not wanting to leave her sister standing alone on the side of the pool.

Luckily the teacher never guessed that any of the children could not jump into the pool. She was already thinking of the next thing she would ask them to do, and fetching a pile of white floats from a store cupboard. While her back was turned, Dawn sat down and slid carefully into the water. It only came up to her chest, even here in the deep end. Lisa slipped in beside her.

"It's all right," said Dawn. "You don't have to wait for me. I'll never manage any of it. You may as well carry on and maybe you can learn to swim properly."

"Two floats each," the teacher was shouting. "Tuck them under your arms, and let's see a nice frog-kick all the way across."

Dawn took the floats and lowered herself in the water. Now she did not feel bigger than usual. Only her head showed above the water, the same as the other children in the class. But she knew that their little legs did not touch the bottom, while she had to bend her legs to keep her shoulders under water. As they kicked their way across the pool, she waded after them, bandy-legged. The water smelt horrible. The other children were swallowing mouthfuls of it, then cheerfully spitting it out again. Dawn felt sick at the thought of getting a drop of it in her mouth.

"Good!" shouted the teacher, as they all reached the other side. "Try and get your legs up behind you, Dawn."

So she had learnt Dawn's name already, although she had not told them her own name.

Not once during that first lesson did Dawn's feet come up off the bottom of the pool. At first Dawn expected the teacher to shout at her, as any of her school teachers would have shouted if she had continually ignored their instructions. But this teacher was not a school teacher. She was used to children who loved swimming and who wanted to learn. No head teacher was going to shout at her if one of her pupils kept both feet on the bottom. She left Dawn alone.

Lisa frog-kicked when the teacher told her to.

She lay on her back and sank, then tried again and floated. She dived to the bottom of the pool to pick up a black brick. The teacher called it a box of chocolates, and the little children laughed and pretended to eat it when they had fetched it from under the water. Lisa dived from the side and went in head first. Dawn watched, and waded about with her legs bent, and longed for the lesson to end. At least the swimming costume did not stretch any more.

Jeff met them outside the changing room. "All right?" he said. "Swimming yet?"

"I swam at least two and a half metres," said Lisa. "And I dived to the bottom and picked up the brick, and I floated on my back. It was great." She looked at Dawn, miserable at her side. "At least, it was all right," she said loyally.

"How about you, Dawn?" Jeff asked.

"It was very nice," said Dawn. She knew that Jeff had spent a lot of money on the lessons, so it was almost like being given a present, and she had to be grateful. She had not dried her hair properly and water was trickling down her neck. She felt terrible. Poppy went past and called out, "Goodbye."

"Cheer up," said Jeff. "You'll soon get the hang of it. I don't think I'll bother to come and watch tomorrow. You can manage without me, can't you?"

"We get a test at the end of the week," said Lisa. "I heard some of the boys saying so. If you pass, you get a badge to sew on your swimming costume. The ten metres badge is purple, and I think five metres is pink, and there's an Honest Swimmer Award as well."

"Honest Swimmer?" said Jeff, laughing. "Are you sure?"

Dawn had overheard the same conversation, and dreaded the coming test. She knew that Lisa meant the Novice Swimmer award, which the boys had said was even easier than the easy-peasy five metres. She thought that she would not even get an Honest Swimmer award, if there were one, because she cheated, with her feet on the bottom.

The swimming lesson had only taken up a little of the morning. All the rest of the day lay ahead, to be filled up somehow before it was time for the next swimming lesson.

"I'll be busy with my marking all day," said Jeff. "But you needn't come straight home with me if you don't want. You can wander around in town if you like, and come home later. I'll give you the bus fare."

He took their damp bundles of swimming things, gave them the money for the bus, and pointed them towards the town centre. "There are some excellent museums," he said. "Shall I tell you how to get to them?"

They waited patiently while he gave directions for three different museums, and at last he crossed the road to get his bus home, swinging his brief-case.

"Look at him skipping along," said Lisa. "He looks really happy, going home to work. He seems to like working better than having time off."

"I expect it's because he's a teacher," said Dawn, as they set off in the opposite direction. "Being with children like us is his usual job, so it seems like work to him."

"But we're his own family," said Lisa. "He should enjoy being with us."

Dawn was relieved that their father did not want to spend the whole time with them. It was a strain to be with him, and she guessed that it was a strain for him too, trying to behave as a father and daughters should behave even though they were nearly strangers. But Lisa wanted him to be her daddy. She thought she knew how daddies should be.

"I'm sure he does enjoy being with us," said Dawn. "I expect he's just worried he won't get the exam papers marked in time."

"There's a park over there," said Lisa after a while. "Let's go and see if it's got any swings."

The park was so large that you couldn't see to the other side. There were benches along the paths. A sign by the gate had a list of rules for people using the park.

"University Parks," read Dawn. "It's probably just for the students."

"It's all universities and colleges here," said Lisa. "Let's go in anyway. They can't own everything."

"Maybe," said Dawn, "but I can't see a playground anyway. We'd better get back to the road. We don't want to get lost."

"We won't get lost," said Lisa. "Come on, let's just explore a little bit."

The path led straight across the grass to a cricket pitch marked off with ropes and surrounded by deck-chairs and benches. No-one was playing. There was a pavilion overlooking the pitch with a scoreboard beside it.

"We'll remember to tell Daddy about this," said Lisa. "He's interested in sport."

Dawn looked behind her, to check that she still remembered the way back. They walked on, crossing another path. Dogs chased each other across the grass.

"Look at that tree," said Lisa. "It looks like the end of a mop."

The tree's branches seemed to start from the top of the tree and slope down all the way to the ground. The branches were so thick that you could not see its trunk at all.

"I'm going inside," called Lisa, and ran off towards the tree.

Dawn looked round first, checking for landmarks so that they would be able to find their way back to the path. When she caught up with Lisa and pushed her way through the branches of the tree into the space inside, Lisa was swinging from a branch and bouncing up and down.

"It's a great camp, isn't it?" said Lisa.

Dawn wondered whether she was still interested in camps. She chose a branch the right height from the ground and tried bouncing on it. She pushed her feet off the ground and let the branch spring her up into the air. She could tell that it was a nice feeling, but even as her legs flew upwards, she felt that the important part of her was still weighted to the ground. It was impossible to forget that Jeff was expecting them to educate themselves before they went back for lunch, and that if they only bounced on trees he would not think much of them as daughters. Disinfected blue swimming pool water gurgled in Dawn's head, and without meaning to, she calculated how many hours were left before the next swimming lesson. About twenty-two. Then the thought that they had left the path and might lose their way into town pulled her down so thoroughly that when her feet touched the ground again, she let go of the branch and let it fly up on its own, shaking down a few leaves.

Lisa hooked her legs over her branch and hung upside-down for a while. "Try this," she said. "The branches grow the right way if you look at them this way up."

Dawn was no good at climbing.

"My glasses would fall off," she said. "We'd better get into town, so that we've seen some of it to tell Jeff about."

"Are you calling him Jeff, then?" asked Lisa.

"I suppose so," said Dawn. "He should have told us what he wanted us to call him, like teachers do at the beginning of the year. 'My name is Mrs Cooper-Smith, and I do not wish to be addressed as Miss'. Come on, let's go and find some old colleges or something."

"There might be a playground further on," said Lisa hopefully, unwinding herself from the branch.

"It's a big park."

"What would a university want a playground for?" said Dawn. "Come on."

They rejoined the path and left the park by the gate they had come in by.

"Those buildings down there look like colleges," said Lisa, pointing further down the road. "They're old, anyway."

"All right, let's try it," said Dawn. She read out the sign on one of the buildings. *"Natural History Museum.* One of Jeff's museums! We'd better go in and notice something to tell him about."

"Do you think we're allowed to?"

They read the sign.

"Open to the public," said Dawn. "We'll just peep in and see if other people are wandering about. You might have to pay. Then we'll tell Jeff why we couldn't go in."

Nobody stopped them at the door or asked them for any money, so they walked up the steps and into the museum.

"I'm going to find something quite a long way in," said Dawn. "In case he's been here. He might know that we had only just been inside the front door."

They wandered up and down the aisles, looking in the glass cases. There were stuffed fish and animals, skeletons and maps of the places where the animals belonged.

"I like armadilloes," said Lisa. "I'll tell him about

armadillos."

There were cases of precious stones and different kinds of rock. Dawn read about volcanoes.

On the way out Lisa stopped to look at the postcard stall.

"We can't buy anything," Dawn reminded her.

"I know," said Lisa. "But it's quicker than looking at the real things."

Jeff was pleased to hear about the museum and the park. He was feeling cheerful because he had got a lot of marking done while the girls were out. There was still plenty left for him to do in the afternoon. There were piles of papers on the round wooden table in the living room, and they had to eat their lunch off their laps, sitting on the big cushions on the floor.

"So you're finding your way around Oxford, then?" he said. "Makes a change from home, doesn't it? Did you get as far as the river in the University Parks?"

"No," said Lisa. "I'd like to see that. Is it a big one, with boats?"

"Big enough for small boats," said Jeff. "People go punting on it, and there are bathing places. There must be a few fish, too. There are always a few people trying to catch them."

"We haven't got a proper river at home," said Lisa. "Not one you can swim in and go in boats."

"We've got the canal," said Dawn. The canal at

home was smelly and full of rubbish, and you never saw a boat on it, but she didn't think it was fair for Jeff to make them agree that Oxford was better than their own home.

"Oh, yes, I remember the canal," said Jeff, and Dawn could tell that he was remembering its dirt and smelliness as well.

"Can we go into town again this afternoon?" Lisa asked.

"I can't afford to keep giving you money for bus fares," said Jeff. "You'll have to amuse yourselves here some of the time. Why don't you play in the garden for a bit, and when I've got through a few more of these papers I'll come down and give you a game of cricket?"

"Have you got a cricket bat?"

"No, I haven't," said Jeff. "I suppose someone downstairs might have one we could borrow. Gordon plays tennis. We could play with a tennis racquet."

"French cricket," said Lisa. "I'm good at that. Mummy plays it with us in the park at home. Sometimes we just use a bit of old wood or something. We played it with Dawn's recorder once."

Dawn liked playing French cricket at home. Mum never threw the ball too hard, and she hit it so that you had a chance of catching it. Dawn guessed that Jeff would want to win, and she was not looking forward to playing with him. She was no good with bats and balls if a game got too serious.

"I'll join you down there later on," said Jeff. "Don't be too noisy. Some of the downstairs people work at home during the day, as well as me."

Dawn and Lisa went down to the garden. There was the big lawn outside the front door, surrounded by tall wild bushes.

"This will be the best place for cricket," said Lisa.

They walked round to the side of the house. There was a small patch of vegetables in neat rows, but you could see that long ago a much larger area had been used as a vegetable garden. A path made of bricks marked out a square near to the kitchen door. Beyond that were more trees and another patch of grass that had been left to grow long and wild.

"I expect they used to have servants to look after the garden," said Dawn. "Head gardeners and under-gardeners and gardeners' boys."

"I don't think Daddy would have had servants," said Lisa, shocked. "He's not that sort of person."

"Not him, silly," said Dawn. "People who lived in this house years ago, when it was a house for just one family. The owners would have used all the big rooms, and the servants would have lived up in Jeff's attic, and worked downstairs in the kitchen." She pointed to a stone outhouse with broken doors. It had some old beds in it and other rubbish, and a few bicycles. "I expect that was the stable. They'd have had a carriage for the posh people, and some of the servants would have had to look after the horses, and drive the carriage and all that."

"I wouldn't have been a servant," said Lisa. "I'd have been one of the grand people, riding in the carriage and having all my vegetables grown for me."

"We'd have been the servants, most likely," said Dawn. "Up in the attic like we are now."

"What can we do?" said Lisa. "We've got nothing to play with."

"We could play tig," said Dawn. "But it's not much good with only two. You always know that the other person has got to get tug in the end. We could play sevens if we had a ball."

"Let's look in the shed," said Lisa. "The old stable. There might be something in there."

They looked at the bicycles padlocked in the shed. There was one smart racing bike, but the rest were old and battered. "Here's a funny one," said Lisa. "It's a bit broken. It's only half a bike."

"There's a lot of junk in here," said Dawn, not really looking.

"I can't see where the other bit came off," said Lisa. "There should be a sharp bit where it broke."

Dawn looked at the broken bicycle. "It's a circus bike," she said. "One of those trick cycles with only one wheel. One of the downstairs people might be a clown."

She thought of the people who had eaten dinner with them the night before. They had all seemed quite ordinary and not like clowns at all. Surely Jeff would have mentioned if one of them had been anything so interesting.

"I'm going to try it," said Lisa. "Hold it up while I get on."

"You can't," said Dawn. "We don't know who it belongs to." But even she didn't feel that it was the same thing as taking an ordinary bicycle that belonged to someone else. Anyone who left something as odd as a unicycle lying around must expect people to try it out. Besides, it wasn't even padlocked.

Lisa wheeled the thing out and put it into Dawn's hands. "I'll lean against the wall," she said, "and hold on to you once I'm on the saddle."

"It's too big for you," said Dawn. "You won't be able to pedal it."

They never found out whether Lisa's legs were long enough to reach the pedals. As soon as she put her weight on the saddle, the cycle tipped. Dawn could not hold it. Lisa fell heavily to the ground and Dawn's hand was caught under the saddle. Lisa screamed.

"Shut up," said Dawn. "You've broken my arm as well. I told you not to try it."

Lisa noticed blood on her elbow and began to cry seriously.

"Stop it," said Dawn. "Everyone will hear you. Let's put it away before someone comes to rescue us. We shouldn't have taken it out."

Quickly Lisa stopped crying, and stood up, snuffling. She tried to pull the unicycle back into the shed, but it seemed more awkward now and its pedals got tangled with the other bicycles.

"Whatever is the matter?" Jeff said. He had come out of the kitchen door and was next to them before they noticed him. "What was all that screaming, and what are you doing in here anyway? Couldn't you play out on the lawn?"

"We were just having a look round," said Dawn, rubbing her twisted arm.

"Are you all right, Lisa?" Jeff asked crossly. She nodded. He noticed the unicycle, half in the shed and half out. "What have you been doing? Taking out bicycles? But they belong to the other people in the house! Have you no respect for other people's property?"

Dawn thought that he sounded very much like a teacher, and felt sorry for the children that he taught at school. Then she felt even more sorry for herself and Lisa, because it must be even worse to have a teacher as a father.

Jeff was inspecting the unicycle. "It must be Sarah's," he said. "She has all sorts of ridiculous things. Look, you have scratched it quite badly here. I don't know what she will say. You will have to apologise."

"I didn't mean to scratch it," sniffed Lisa. "I only wanted to try it out. It wasn't padlocked."

"So nothing is safe from you unless it's under lock and key?" snorted Jeff. "I'd have thought you knew better than that! You can explain to Sarah that you didn't mean this and that. Do you know which room is hers?"

"I think I do," said Dawn. "I saw her go in to it on the first morning. It's next to the bathroom."

"Right," said Jeff grimly. "And make it a proper apology. You had better tell her that I'll pay to repair the damage. Now I'll get back to my marking."

He lifted the unicycle and placed it carefully at the back of the shed against the old bedsteads, then went indoors. Dawn and Lisa waited until he had had time to get upstairs, then wandered round to the lawn in front of the house, by the front door.

"We'd better go and do it," said Dawn. "He'll know if we don't."

"What am I supposed to say?" asked Lisa, looking scared. "I don't know how to apologise, when a person doesn't even know what you've done wrong. I can't just say sorry."

"Just say you were playing with her bike and you fell off and it got a bit scratched," said Dawn. "She didn't look horrible. If you keep on sniffing she'll probably feel sorry for you."

"You were holding the bike as well," said Lisa. "You say it. I can't."

"It was your stupid idea," said Dawn. "Anyone could see that it was far too big for you to ride, and even if it was your size, you don't know how to ride a bike with only one wheel."

A loud bang made them jump. Jeff had knocked on the glass of the attic window. He was looking down at them. Dawn nodded to him and went inside.

"Come on," she said to Lisa. "He's waiting for you to apologise."

They went upstairs to the first floor landing.

"I can't," said Lisa.

"I'll knock for you," said Dawn. "Then you say it."

She knocked on the door that she thought was Sarah's. Much too quickly Sarah opened the door. "Hello," she said, looking very friendly. "Jeff busy, is he? Do you want to come in?"

They went into the room but left the door open, because she would probably want them to leave quickly once she heard that they had damaged her unicycle.

Lisa said nothing. Dawn nudged her, but it did not work.

"We came to apologise," said Dawn. "We found your bike in the shed, the one with one wheel, and it fell over while we were looking at it and it got scratched but Jeff says he'll pay to have it fixed up. I'm very sorry."

She nudged Lisa again, and this time she muttered "Sorry" as well. Sarah looked rather surprised.

"Is it really damaged?" she asked. "Or just scratched? Because I think it was quite scratched already. Everyone just throws their bicycles into that shed, and they all get a bit battered. Except for Simon, of course. His is the racing bike, and he insists on having one wall to himself to lean his bike against. But that unicycle is scratched all over, and your father is probably one of the people who chucks his bike on top of it. In fact he may well have made the scratch that you noticed." She laughed. "Do you want to have a go on it?" she asked. "You need someone holding you on each side when you first try it."

"I think Lisa's legs are too short," said Dawn.

Sarah looked at Lisa measuringly. "They might be. But Dawn might just manage it. The saddle is adjustable, you know."

Now that Sarah was turning out to be so friendly, Lisa decided that she had not apologised thoroughly enough. "I'm very sorry," she said. "I didn't mean to."

"It doesn't matter," said Sarah. It seemed that it really didn't. "Come down and you can have another try. It is hard until you get the knack. You know how to ride an ordinary bike, do you?"

"Can I just look at this?" Lisa asked. She had noticed something on Sarah's desk.

"Stop it," whispered Dawn. "You'll break something else."

But Sarah had picked the something up and was explaining it to Lisa.

It was a brightly-coloured tin whale with a tiny tin fish attached to it by a string. Sarah knelt on the floor and ran the fish along the carpet. It had tiny wheels under it. Then she let it go and it rattled along. Gradually the whale caught up with the fish and at last snapped it up in its mouth and swallowed it. Lisa picked it up and looked inside the mouth. There was the fish, undigested. Lisa pulled it out, ready to be swallowed again.

"Why do you have toys?" she asked.

"Why not?" said Sarah. "Look, this one is nice too." She fetched a box from a high shelf and took out a little tin roundabout. When she wound it up, it turned with a jangling metallic sound, and three tiny aeroplanes flew round it in a circle. "What I like about this one is the instructions," she said. *"Wind the key and the flying of aeronauts will be entrancingly seen.* They translate it from Chinese and they never get it quite right."

Dawn looked at the book shelves which covered two walls of the room completely. The books had been pushed to the back of the shelves, and more books were stacked in piles in front of them, or wedged into the gaps above them. There were a lot of toys on the shelves as well, balanced in front of the books. Dawn saw a metal bird that she liked. It had a key sticking out from its side, and she wondered whether it could fly, or only hop. There was a lantern as well, a barometer, a vase of flowers that looked as though they had been dead for a long time and a lot of cups.

"It's a mess, isn't it?" said Sarah. "Give me a hand clearing up all these old cups of tea, would you?"

Dawn reached up for a cup. She thought it would

be empty. There were such a lot of them all round the room. But it was full of cold tea, perhaps from days ago, and much heavier than she had expected. Also it was stuck to the shelf, and came off with a jerk in Dawn's hand. The tea spilt down her front and on to a pile of papers lying on the floor.

Sarah mopped it up carelessly with something that looked like a shirt. "I should drink it when I make it," she said. "It's always getting spilt. I like the idea of a nice cup of tea, and I like warming my hands on the cup, but it's always too hot to drink straight away, and then I forget about it."

"You could mix it with cold water as soon as you've made it," suggested Lisa. "Then it would be cool enough to drink straight away."

"That's a good idea," said Sarah, looking surprised. "I never thought of that."

They carried the cups carefully downstairs. Lisa and Dawn took two each and Sarah carried the rest on a large atlas which served as a tray.

"Coming to try the unicycle, then?" said Sarah.

Lisa was outside, already trying to lift the unicycle out from behind the other bicycles.

"There's the scratch," said Dawn. "But Jeff did say that he would pay to have it fixed."

"That scratch has always been there," said Sarah. "Look at it, there is paint chipped off all over. And your father is as bad as the rest of them, chucking his bike into the shed."

"I didn't even know he had a bike," said Dawn.

"Just a minute," said Sarah. She went round to the lawn and stood in the middle of it with her hands on her hips, facing the house. "Jeff!" she shouted at the top of her voice. "Jeff!"

"She's going to tell him off for scratching the bike," whispered Lisa. They hid inside the shed until Sarah came back.

She was smiling. "He's pretending he can't hear me," she said. "I can see him sitting at his table up there, but he won't look up from his books. Never mind, let's have a go at this bike."

Sarah held the unicycle upright near to the wall while Lisa scrambled on.

"Hold on round both our necks," said Sarah. "Dawn, try and get round the other side of her. Now, just pedal."

But Lisa's legs were too short.

"Come on, then, Dawn," said Sarah. "You have a go."

Dawn heaved herself up on the unicycle while Sarah strained to keep it steady. Clinging on to Sarah on one side and Lisa on the other, Dawn began to pedal. A bicycle can fall in either of two directions, both painful. A unicycle can fall in more than a million different directions. Dawn pedalled, and the cycle crossed the lawn, but only because Sarah was holding it, and Dawn, up. Dawn slid to the ground and watched as Sarah climbed onto the unicycle, hanging on to a tree to get herself up.

"You can really do it!" said Lisa. "I didn't know

that ordinary people could really ride them. Can I have another go?"

Sarah rode in a small wobbly circle and came back to the tree, almost falling off. "I'm no good at it really," she said. "I bought it because I thought it would be handy for getting through the traffic in town. I thought, no hands, so I can carry all my shopping or my brief-case or whatever, and still make hand-signals. But I don't think I'd ever be steady enough to ride on the road, and anyway you need both hands for getting on and off."

Dawn imagined riding down the High Street on a unicycle, with an armful of carrier bags, whistling a carefree tune as people on the pavements stopped to stare.

"I know what's better for zooming around with lots of shopping," said Lisa. "A skateboard. Me and Dawn have got one at home, and Mum makes me take it when I go down to the shops. You do need one hand free to pick it up when you go across roads, but you can carry the shopping in the other hand. And some people even skateboard on the road."

Dawn and Sarah lifted Lisa on to the unicycle again and pushed her round the lawn. The pedals swung round and hit Dawn on the shins.

"I'd better go and get on with a bit more work," said Sarah. "Shall I put it away, or do you want to go on playing with it?"

"Better put it away," said Dawn. "We couldn't

manage it on our own. Thanks for letting us try it."

"I'll tell Jeff it was him that put that scratch on it," said Sarah, as she went indoors.

"Do you think she will?" Lisa asked.

Later on, they decided that she had, because when Jeff came out to play French cricket with them, he bowled so fiercely that they were out every time, and it was no fun at all.

Chapter

≈ 8 ≈

Dawn was still in bed when Jeff came in from his morning run the next day. She was putting off waking up because it would bring the swimming lesson nearer. She heard a door slam far downstairs, and a little later his feet came thundering up the wooden staircase.

"Daddy's coming!" said Lisa, who was dressed already. "You had better get up quick."

"Shh, I'm asleep," said Dawn, wishing that she was. She had had a nice dull dream about something ordinary. It might have been school, or going shopping with Mum, she could not quite remember, but she would have liked to get back into it.

"Come on, lazybones!" said Jeff, as he burst into the living room in his shorts and bare feet. He was running on the spot, holding his soggy trainers and socks in one hand. "It's a lovely day. It poured with rain in the night and everything is sparkling. Come on, get up."

He jogged away to his bedroom to change into his daytime clothes. Dawn sat up and put on her glasses. She began to think that it was too late to wish that the swimming lesson would never arrive. Now she would just have to wish that it would soon be over. To hurry it along she got dressed and washed quickly, tidied the bed and had her cereal poured out before Lisa.

"So what do you two like to spend your time doing at home?" Jeff asked. It sounded as though he was carrying on a conversation that had already been started, but it did not follow on from anything they had talked about before. Dawn imagined that while he was jogging his mile that morning he had thought, time I got to know more about the girls. And here he was getting to know about them. She said nothing.

"Anything," said Lisa.

"What about school? What subjects do you like best?"

"I don't do subjects," said Lisa. "It's all integrated."

"But what do you like doing best? Sport, maths, art?"

"I like free study best, really," said Lisa. "It's what you do when you've finished your work."

"You choose what to study then, do you?" asked Jeff. "So what do you choose?"

"I just talk to my friends," said Lisa.

Jeff gave up on Lisa. "What about you, Dawn?" he asked.

"I'm good at maths and geography and history," said Dawn. "At least, those are what I get the best marks for."

"History?" said Jeff, and his eyes lit up. "That's

great. Do you remember all those stories I used to tell you about the Greeks and Romans, when you were little?"

Dawn smiled and nodded, hoping that he would not ask her about the stories. She had one very clear memory of trying to wriggle off his knee as he tried to tell her about some very important battle, but probably some of the stories had been quite interesting.

"I tell you what," said Jeff. "If I get on well with my work tomorrow, how about us spending tomorrow afternoon in town, and we'll go to the Ashmolean? It's a great place for history."

"What sort of Shmolean?" asked Lisa.

"Ashmolean," said Jeff. "It's a museum. You'll love it, Dawn, if you are interested in history."

It was too late to say that she was not particularly interested in history. She was just good at it.

"If the weather's like this," Jeff said, "it will be a perfect day for looking round Oxford. Look at that sky!" They had to bend down to look at the sky through the low attic window. "What about you, Lisa? What would you like to do in town?"

"I'd like to go to a nice restaurant and have a pizza and chips."

"Well, we'll see," said Jeff. Dawn thought he was disappointed that Lisa had not begged to go to two museums instead of just one.

"Mummy never takes us to restaurants," said Lisa.

"She took us to McDonalds for your birthday," said Dawn, "and three of your greedy little friends." She did not mean to let Lisa start a competition between Mummy and Jeff.

"Yes, but she never normally takes us," said Lisa.

"Well, if I take you it won't be normal," said Jeff. "I warn you, I'm not made of money."

Later Jeff took them to the bus stop and told them to ask the driver to put them off at the swimming pool. In the bus Lisa asked, "Is Jeff richer than Mummy or not?"

"Of course he is," said Dawn. "People who get long holidays always earn more money than people who only get four weeks a year."

"Then why doesn't he live in a proper house, and have a car and a video and go to restaurants every day?"

"Maybe he hasn't had time to buy them yet," said Dawn. "He hasn't been back from Australia very long. And some people don't want cars and videos."

Lisa thought about that for a while. "I don't think he can be rich," she said at last. "He can't even afford to give us bus money twice a day. Maybe he teaches at a very poor school and they don't pay him very much at all."

"His new school in England won't have started paying him yet," said Dawn. "He hasn't started working there yet, has he? And the school he was teaching at in Australia probably stopped paying him when he left. So maybe he hasn't any money at all at the moment. But once he starts getting paid he'll have much more money than Mum."

Dawn rang the bell, and they got up and stood next to the driver, so that she would not forget to stop at the swimming pool.

"I think he didn't come with us this morning so that he would save on the bus fare," Lisa went on, as they climbed down on to the pavement.

"He just wanted to get on with his work," said Dawn. "Anyway, it doesn't matter. Just don't keep on asking him to buy you things, or he will think that Mum hasn't brought us up to be polite."

"I only said pizza and chips because he asked what I would like," said Lisa. Now they were at the sports centre. "That's what I would like, and I saw two pizza places when we were in town yesterday."

"He meant old buildings and things like that," said Dawn. "But it doesn't matter."

Now they shut themselves away from the sharp sunshine and dazzling wet pavements. They were in the hot changing room, and Dawn had no more energy for talking. The tiled floor had been washed with strong-smelling disinfectant. Some small children were throwing their vests at each other, and two mothers were talking about how their children's strokes had improved, and how one of them should have got its badge last term, but the teacher hadn't realised what progress it had made.

"It's just that he won't concentrate. I know he can do the hundred metres, but he's got to make that extra bit of effort."

"I don't think they pay enough attention to the style. I mean, Tasha's got her hundred metres, but you can hardly call it crawl, what she does, it's more a sort of doggy-paddle really, and I think it's the teacher's job to see to that, don't you?"

"I told Graham that he'll have a pound if he gets the badge next time. I just think he needs to be pushed."

Dawn wondered whether these children enjoyed their lessons. It did not sound much fun, being pushed and making extra effort and having to be bribed to swim, and yet the children seemed cheerful enough.

One woman was saying to her daughter, "It's Marie's birthday tomorrow. See if you can swim all the way across today, for her birthday. All the way across on your front, as a birthday present."

Dawn watched as the little girl kissed her baby sister goodbye. The baby must be Marie! How could swimming across the pool be a birthday present for her? Dawn thought some of these mothers were a bit mad. Lisa was changed first, and joined a group of children standing in the foot-bath waiting for the lesson to begin.

"Hello," said Poppy, bursting into the changing room and throwing her bag down on a bench. "Am I late? Oh no, they haven't gone in yet. Did you like it yesterday? I didn't see you after the lesson, because my teacher kept me afterwards to do some diving. I used to have your teacher when I first came. She's a bit strict, isn't she? Did Lisa like it?"

Poppy had come with her swimming costume on underneath her clothes, and she was changed in a minute. Dawn saw her talking to Lisa as they paddled in the foot-bath. Dawn put her glasses inside her shoe and locked her clothes away. Then she followed Lisa and Poppy and joined the crowd of children who were laughing and jumping around and splashing each other while they waited for their lessons to begin. Suddenly a whistle was blown and everyone went through to wait by the side of the pool.

"Bye," said Poppy. "See you afterwards." She went to stand against the wall by the deep pool, with the other big children. Dawn and Lisa stood awkwardly with the little children.

"How old are you?" one of them asked Dawn.

"Five," said Dawn. "I'm big for my age, aren't I?"

The child looked up at her, frowning. "I don't believe you, actually," she said, and went to talk to someone else.

"Poppy knows about that park we went to yesterday," said Lisa. "She's got a canoe there. She told me where it was. Can we go and look for it when we've finished here?"

"Is Poppy going there as well?" asked Dawn.

"No," said Lisa. "I asked her to, but she said she has to go home. Her mother waits for her to get back. She said after all that rain in the night the canoe would be full of water, so I said we would empty it out for her. Poppy's nice, isn't she?"

"Is that her class diving over there?" said Dawn. "Watch."

The children in Poppy's group were standing on the edge of the deep pool, arms straight above their heads and knees bent. The teacher walked along behind them and touched them, one at a time, on the shoulder. As he touched them, they dived. Some of them fell in like spiders, some flopped like mattresses, but Poppy cut through the water like a knife.

"Here comes our teacher," said Lisa.

The teacher marked the children off on her register and led them to the far end of the little pool.

"Everybody in!" she shouted.

Dawn sat down and slithered quickly into the water. It was warm, like a bath. Without her glasses on, everything seemed a little unreal.

"Come on," said the teacher in her loud, jolly voice. "Let's see a nice jump."

She was looking at Dawn. Dawn had to pull herself back up out of the water. She felt like a clumsy seal struggling on to a rock as she heaved herself up on to the tiled edge of the pool. The other children were already in the water, and Lisa had jumped in as well. Dawn stood up and looked down into the blue water. She knew that if she jumped down into it she would never come up again.

"Come along," said the teacher. "You managed it

yesterday! Not frightened, are you, a big girl like you?"

Dawn jumped. It was no further than jumping off the wall outside her school, which she had often done, and the water made the landing softer. Her feet touched the bottom before the water reached her face, and she was standing in the water. Quickly she bent her legs until her shoulders were under water. It had not been so bad. She wondered whether the teacher would praise her, or jeer at her for having been frightened, but the teacher had moved on to the next thing, which was handing out white floats to everyone.

"Hold the float behind your head," she was saying. "Lie back and kick with your legs. Not so hard, Katie, please!"

Dawn kept her feet on the bottom, and her mouth tightly closed, and survived the second swimming lesson.

"Well?" said Lisa when they were nearly dressed. "Shall we go and see Poppy's canoe?"

Poppy was swinging her bag over her shoulder, ready to leave.

"Do go and have a look," she said. "It's a lovely place, where we keep it. There's a weir, and a bridge, and a pool where you can swim, and loads of moorhens."

"I don't think it can be the same park that we went to," said Dawn. "We didn't see any river. It was just grass and trees and a cricket pitch."

"That's right," said Poppy. "And there are tennis courts as well. You have to go past all that, and then you get to the river."

"Come and show us the way," said Lisa. "Your mum won't mind."

"She will," said Poppy. "She worries about me. I'll have to go now. But we could meet there another day. She doesn't mind if she knows where I am. What about tomorrow?"

"Jeff's meeting us after swimming tomorrow," said Dawn.

"He's taking us to a museum," said Lisa, "because Dawn said she liked history. What about

Thursday, then? You could teach us to canoe.''

"It's not very safe if you can't swim," said Poppy. "But let's go there anyway. I'll tell Mummy. Look, I'll have to go now. See you tomorrow. 'Bye!"

"I will be able to swim by Thursday!" Lisa called after her.

"Did she tell you how to find the place?" Dawn asked.

"Sort of," said Lisa. "I'm sure I can find it. Come on."

The walk to the park where they had been the day before seemed shorter this time, because they knew where they were going. The pavements had dried off and only a few puddles were left, reflecting blue if you looked at them from the right angle. A gusty wind dried their hair as they walked, and blew the clouds fast across the sky. After the blur of the swimming pool, now that Dawn had her glasses on again everything looked particularly crisp. The dangling round seed-heads on the plane trees looked as though they had been drawn on with a pencil, each one so neat and clear.

"Past the cricket pitch, she said," said Lisa. "Head for the far corner of the park. A path between some hedges. That must be it."

They found the river. It had several branches, dividing and passing under different bridges. The path wound over them and led on among tall trees.

"This is the place," said Lisa. "She said there was a plank bridge over a weir. Is that a weir?"

"I think so," said Dawn. The weir was like a hand-made waterfall. Water gushed down a concrete slope to a pool below, and then swirled away down one of the little rivers. "Do they swim here, then? With the water gushing like that? It doesn't look very safe."

"Poppy says it's more fun swimming in moving water," said Lisa. "I'm going across the bridge."

The bridge at the top of the weir was no more than a thick plank raised about half a metre above the level of the water. There was a hand-rail beside it.

"You'd better not," said Dawn. "If you fell in, you'd be taken all the way down to the sea. I couldn't rescue you."

"No, but I won't fall," said Lisa. "I'll hold on to the rail." She set off along the plank. Dawn could see that it really was wide and sturdy enough to be perfectly safe.

"It makes you giddy to look down," shouted Lisa. "Look at the water gushing underneath your feet."

There was no need for her to shout, but it made her feel as though she was in a more distant and dangerous place. Dawn went a little way along the bridge and watched the water slide away under her.

"I'm coming back now," called Lisa. "I'm going to look for the canoe. Shall I climb round you?"

"No," said Dawn. "I'll go back first."

They reached solid ground again.

"We'll come here every day as soon as I can swim

ten metres," said Lisa. "That pool at the bottom looks quite deep. Poppy can teach me how to dive."

"Where does she keep her canoe?" Dawn asked.

"Tall grass somewhere. Two trees, she said. By the fence." Lisa looked around, and then set off. "It's here! I've found it!"

"It's not very well hidden, is it?" said Dawn. "Anybody could come and steal it."

"We wouldn't have found it if we hadn't known about it," said Lisa. "And there aren't any oars or anything, so nobody could get anywhere in it."

"You use paddles in a canoe, not oars," said Dawn.

"You don't use anything, if you haven't got them," said Lisa. "It has got a bit of water in. Come and help me tip it out."

"They should leave it upside down," said Dawn. "Why don't they? Then it wouldn't get rain-water in it."

They discovered why, when they tipped the canoe over to let out the water. While the top of the canoe was a plain brown colour, the underneath was white, which would show up much too brightly through the grass. It was hard to get all the water out. It slopped from one end of the canoe to the other, but did not want to come out of the hole in the middle, the hole where the canoeist would sit.

"Let's lift it up and shake it around," said Lisa. "Then it will have to come out."

They each took an end and lifted the canoe right

out of its hiding place.

"Come out into the open, then," said Dawn, "or it will get bashed against the fence."

They swung the canoe between them and some of the water splashed out.

"It's not as heavy as I thought it would be," said Lisa. "I wonder what it's made of?"

They looked at the shiny white underneath of the canoe.

"It looks hairy," said Dawn. "It's got threads in it. Or bits of grass."

"Threads!" said Lisa. "Perhaps it's a knitted canoe."

Suddenly, above the mixed rushing and rustling sound of the water tumbling over the weir and the trees overhead shaking in the wind, they heard a shout. Someone was yelling at someone else. Dawn and Lisa looked up to see what was going on. Some children must be having a quarrel.

A tall girl on the other side of the river was screaming, "Put that down! Get away from it! That's ours!"

A smaller girl shouted, "You keep an eye on them, Di. I'll run round by the bridge."

It was Dawn and Lisa that they were shouting at, for touching the canoe. The tall girl stood with her hands on her hips, leaning forward and glaring at them, as though she was daring them to move. The other girl had disappeared, running at top speed.

Lisa dropped her end of the canoe.

"Don't just drop it," said Dawn. "Quick, put it back, and then we'll get away. We can't just leave it here, and let them steal it. We should find a new hiding place for it, really."

Hurriedly they pushed the canoe back in its nest of flattened grass against the fence. Dawn pulled a few of the tallest grasses up to hide it again.

"Come on!" said Lisa. "Run!" She grabbed her swimming bag and set off down the path that led back across the park. Dawn followed.

"But they'll take the canoe," she protested, following Lisa. "What will we tell Poppy?"

"Didn't you see who they were?" panted Lisa over her shoulder. "It was those girls from the tower where we met Poppy! I think they must be cousins or maybe step-sisters. They don't live with her all the time. The little one was called Jenny."

"The other one was called Diane," said Dawn. "I didn't know it was them. It's probably their canoe as well, then." They came to the tree with the thick hanging branches that they had swung on the day before. "Here, let's get into your tree camp and hide for a bit. I'm out of breath. We can watch through the leaves and see if they come. I didn't recognise them, yelling at us like that across the river. But then I didn't expect to recognise them, so I didn't look at them properly." Dawn leant against the trunk of the tree, pleased to have found such a safe hiding place. "But if you knew who they were, why did we run away? Why didn't you say that Poppy asked us to empty the canoe?"

"It was you that said we should get away," said Lisa.

"I wonder why they didn't recognise us?" said Dawn. "You're even wearing the same clothes you were wearing when we met them on Saturday. You'd better put clean ones on tomorrow."

"Well, you didn't recognise them either," said Lisa. "And now they think we're robbers, trying to steal their canoe."

"I hope we don't have to meet them again," said Dawn. "It would be really embarrassing."

"Shh," said Lisa. "Here she comes. She took a long time."

Dawn peeped out from between the branches. The younger girl came jogging slowly along the path towards the weir. Now Dawn could see it was Jenny, the girl that had been at the top of the tower with Poppy on that first morning. She was frowning.

"We could just go out and explain," Dawn whispered doubtfully.

"All right," said Lisa. "You can if you want."

Dawn did not want to. Jenny disappeared between two hedges. She would be at the weir in a minute, checking the canoe for damage.

"We'd better go," said Dawn. "They might start looking round for us."

"Which way?" whispered Lisa. "Shall we go somewhere new, to throw them off the trail?"

"Silly," answered Dawn. "They don't know what our normal way is anyway. And if we go anywhere new, we'll get lost. Straight across the park to the gate, and then we'll head into town. I'm going to take my sweater off, so that I'll look different if they see us from a distance. Take yours off too, and shove it in your bag. Hurry up. The big one will know which way we set off."

"She's called Diane," said Lisa. "You shouldn't talk about her as though she's an enemy. She didn't know we were friends."

They crept out from between the dangling branches and sprinted across the grass, then strolled casually, but fast, along the path, looking like someone else. Outside the gate they slowed down, panting a little.

"They probably won't bother chasing us," said Dawn. "Jenny will canoe over to fetch Diane, and then they'll get on with doing whatever it was they came there for."

They watched anxiously through the railings, but saw no sign of the two girls coming after them.

"I'm freezing," said Lisa.

"Let's go and get warm," said Dawn.

They chose a big department store, where no-one was likely to ask them what they wanted to buy. They looked at the clothes and toys, and let someone spray some perfume on their wrists. Then they discovered the new shopping centre, and Lisa decided that it was the best part of Oxford that they had found so far. It had a smooth floor of different coloured polished stone, cleaner than an ordinary pavement because it was indoors. Set in the high ceiling were mirrors.

"Look, I'm floating up there," Lisa called out, and walked slowly along the wide mall between the shop fronts with her head tilted back, to see herself hanging upside-down from the other pavement high in the air. Dawn liked the mirrors too, but after she had bumped into a brisk impatient man in a suit, because of looking up instead of along, she concentrated on steering Lisa instead of gazing at her own reflection.

Jeff was pleased to hear about the mirrors in the shopping centre, because Dawn had noticed the strange things that happened where the mirror on one of the walls met the one on the ceiling; and that was maths, or perhaps physics.

On Wednesday morning they were more than half-way through the week of swimming lessons. It had seemed such a long time, stretching ahead, but now it was just a handful of unpleasant hours, three finished and gone, with only two still to come. The lessons had not got any better, but they no longer had to fill up the whole of Dawn's life.

Dawn hated walking on the floor of the changing room. Either it was dirty from all the dampened shoes that had walked on it, or it smelt of fresh disinfectant. The teacher never ran out of ideas. There was swimming backwards and forwards, jumping and diving from the side, diving to fetch a brick that the teacher had thrown to the bottom of the pool, pushing off from the side and gliding with your face down. For most of it you were meant to get your face wet. Dawn did not want to get her face wet. She shut her eyes and mouth tight, but the smell and taste of the water got in through every crack.

Now the end of the week was in sight.

"Are you enjoying it at all?" Poppy asked as they dried themselves after Wednesday's lesson. "I wish you could have been in my group."

"I love it," said Lisa. "I really can swim now. The teacher said she would take us in the big pool tomorrow to try for our ten metres."

"You could come canoeing, then," said Poppy. "You have to be able to swim in case the canoe tips up."

"Oh, no," said Dawn. "I mean, she isn't that good yet."

Lisa giggled. "We met your sisters yesterday," she said. "They chased us away."

"Do you mean Diane and Jenny?" said Poppy, puzzled. "Where? Why would they chase you?"

"It didn't matter," said Dawn. "It was a misunderstanding, that's all. We didn't recognise each other, and they thought we were just strangers messing about with your canoe."

"We were tipping the water out, like you asked us to," said Lisa. "Diane shouted at us, so we ran away."

"Why didn't you just explain who you were?" Poppy asked. "They would have remembered as soon as they looked at you properly. But we have had people messing about with the boat before, so I suppose you can't blame them. It's not a very safe place to leave it, but it's too far to carry it all the way from home every time we need it. In term-time we just take it there at week-ends."

"Anyway, Dawn never wants to go there again," said Lisa, "in case she meets your fierce sisters."

"You were running as fast as me," said Dawn. "I

only said it would be embarrassing, with them thinking we were burglars or something."

"I'll come with you next time," said Poppy. "I don't usually see them during the week because they live with their mother, so I can't explain to them before Saturday. But if I'm there with you it will be all right. They aren't really horrible, Diane and Jenny. Not most of the time. And you'll see, it's great fun with the canoe. What about tomorrow? We could bring a picnic. I'll fix it up with my mum."

It was arranged, and they hurriedly got dressed.

"The others might not be there tomorrow anyway," said Lisa, as they left the changing room.

"Come on," said Dawn. "Jeff will be waiting for us."

Jeff was pleased with the amount of work he had got done while the girls were swimming and exploring Oxford, and he was waiting for them, full of energy for their visit to the museum.

The Ashmolean had wide steps up to its front entrance. Lisa jumped backwards up them.

"I hope you know how to behave in a museum," said Jeff.

Dawn thought that they should line up in twos, like on a school trip, but nobody would have noticed because there were only two of her and Lisa anyway.

Inside the front door was a stall selling postcards and books.

"Can we buy something?" said Lisa, hanging back

to look at the books.

"Come on," said Jeff impatiently. "We came to see the things in the museum, not photographs of them." He stood in front of a large plan of the museum. "What shall we look at first?" he said. "Dawn, what do you think would be most interesting?"

Dawn looked at the squares which were the different rooms in the museum, and read the words written in them. *XIIth century silverware, XIVth century.*

"I don't mind," she said.

"Let's go upstairs," said Lisa. She was already half-way up the wide marble staircase, leaning over the balustrade. The others followed her up.

"I can't remember what's up here," said Jeff.

At the top of the stairs was a small glass case with a model building inside it. "A dolls' house!" called Lisa.

It was a model of a Roman villa, with different buildings and rooms and a few figures of people in togas. It was not as interesting as Dawn at first hoped. There were small trees, and they had made a shiny place to show where the water was, but somehow it did not look real enough. The grass was flat green furry stuff, all the same dull green. You could not tell from looking at it what it would have been like to live in a house like that.

"I've seen the original of this one," said Jeff. "Only the site, of course. You can't see much except the foundations. But it's fascinating the way they arranged their living quarters. So civilised, to have those big communal baths."

Dawn thought that communal baths sounded disgusting. She imagined the swimming pool, full of soapy water and hair. It was bad enough having to share the bath water at home with Lisa and her dirty knees. Communal baths would be even worse than the blue pool water smelling of chemicals.

"Come on," said Lisa, pulling Jeff by the arm.

The next room had dull pictures in golden frames on the walls, and a grand chair in each corner. Lisa immediately flopped down in one of the chairs, a hand on each padded velvet arm. Before she had arranged herself to feel like a princess, Jeff hauled her up out of it.

"For God's sake, child!" he said in a low voice. He did not want the museum attendants to notice that anything was wrong. "This is a museum, not your mother's living room!"

Dawn thought that there was no reason to mention Mum, unless he was criticising her in some way. Perhaps he meant that it was all right to behave badly in Mum's house.

Lisa was not upset. "This is all boring pictures," she said. "Look, through there I can see some real things."

They followed her into the next section. A woman in a dark uniform was strolling through the rooms with her hands behind her back. Dawn saw that Jeff was blushing. He hustled the two girls into a side room. "Let's look at this room properly," he said. "There's no point in just rushing round from room to room. Read some of the labels." He began to read one of the labels out loud.

"This is Guy Fawkes' real lantern," said Dawn.

Lisa came to look. "It's a bit shabby," she said.

Jeff rolled his eyes. "Well," he said, "it is more than three hundred years old. There's a fascinating room downstairs. Egyptian amulets. You'll love them. Lots of little cats and monkeys, Lisa."

Before she followed Jeff and Lisa to the stairs, Dawn stood on tiptoe to peep inside a huge clay jar. It was empty. There were cracks in its reddish-grey sides, and she wondered if it had been dug up out of the ground in broken scraps, and pieced together by someone who knew what shape it should make. She laid her hand on the cool outside of the jar. It was not quite smooth. The museum attendant came and stood behind her and she quickly put her hand in her pocket and joined the others.

Downstairs they met something strange. Jeff pretended that nothing was odd. He marched to a glass case and looked inside, frowning. But in the serious quietness of the museum, a young woman was saying, not loudly but quite clearly, "Good! Come on, then, Danny! You can do it!"

Who could Danny be? What could anyone do in a museum except be quiet? Dawn and Lisa looked around. Coming along the smooth floor, which was patterned with different-coloured marble, was a small boy. He was crawling, but he looked much too big to be crawling. He was as big as some of the children in the swimming class. Why did his mother not tell him to stand up, walk properly, and be quiet? And look properly in the glass cases, and read the labels?

"I think he's handicapped," Lisa whispered to Dawn.

"Shh," said Dawn, in case the mother heard. She looked more carefully at the boy, and decided that Lisa was right. He looked straight back up at Dawn from his awkward position on the floor, and she could see that his face was crooked and his head tilted to one side. There was a big smile across his face, but Dawn did not notice that. She looked away, because it seemed more polite than staring at him. She went to look at an Egyptian amulet.

"Come on, Danny! Just once more round and you've done it!" the woman was calling. The boy's arms looked thin and tired, but he lifted his head and crawled towards his mother. When he reached the Egyptian mummy, his mother picked him up and hugged him. He was thin, and probably not very heavy.

"That was fantastic!" she said, and kissed him on the cheek. "You're great! Five times round! Let's go and look at the monkeys now."

The boy bounced in her arms and waved towards the cases that Jeff was looking in. Dawn and Lisa went and looked in them too, to show Jeff that they were interested. They wanted to see the monkeys that the boy was so pleased to be shown. The monkeys were small and made of metal. One of them had its tail curled round to make a loop.

"You could hang it round your neck on a string," said Lisa.

"That's right," said Jeff. "They were good-luck charms. I expect they were hung round people's necks to protect them from evil."

"Look at this little monster," said Lisa. "It's got a really funny face."

"It's a god," said Dawn, reading the label.

"It doesn't look much like God to me," said Lisa.

"Come on, then, Danny," the woman was saying. "Five more times before we go home."

She carried the little boy back to the room where he had been crawling before, and put him down on the floor. He made a cross mewing sound and did not move.

"Come on, Danny boy! You can do it! Then we'll go home on the bus, and you can ring the bell!"

Perhaps Danny liked buses, or bells. Slowly he began to crawl. He crawled up one side of the long room, past the old bronze age weapons, and back down the other side by the Anglo-Saxon armour. It took him a long time. It was an effort for him to move each hand forward, and an effort to make each knee follow it.

"Why does she make him do it?" Lisa whispered to Dawn. "You can see he's tired out."

"Perhaps she's trying to get him fit," said Dawn.

Jeff called them away to see something else, an Egyptian tomb guarded by carved dogs with curly faces. When they left the museum the little boy had gone.

"What did you think of it?" Jeff asked as they went down the wide stone steps. Lisa was jumping down them two steps at a time. "We're lucky to have a good museum like that, right on our doorstep, aren't we? What did you think was the most interesting part?"

"I liked the light switches," said Lisa. "I've never seen any like that before."

"I liked the big pots upstairs," said Dawn.

"Pots?" said Jeff. "What pots were those? Where did they come from?"

"I don't know," said Dawn. Jeff had rushed her away before she had time to look at them properly.

"Hmm," said Jeff. "It doesn't sound as though either of you learnt much from the museum, then."

"Why do you suppose that woman was making her little boy crawl all round the museum, Daddy?" Lisa asked.

"What little boy?" said Jeff, carefully sounding careless.

"There was a little handicapped boy crawling along near the Egyptian things. His mother made him go ten times round the room."

"How extraordinary," said Jeff. "I can't imagine why."

Dawn thought that he must have noticed the little boy and wondered why he was pretending not to have seen him.

"Are we going to have a pizza now, Daddy? Can we?" Lisa asked.

"Food seems to be the only thing that you two girls are interested in," grumbled Jeff. "All right, then, let's find a pizza place. You say you are interested in history, and then all you look at in the museum is the light switches, for goodness' sake. What *are* you interested in?"

Dawn tried to think what she was interested in. She thought that Jeff meant school subjects, and there certainly were not very many school subjects that she was interested in. But at home she was never bored, so it couldn't be that she was interested in nothing.

"Here's the place, Daddy!" Lisa called out. "I want to go in this one! It's got twelve different sorts of pizza!"

The restaurant was downstairs. The front entrance opened on to the top of a winding iron staircase that led down to a green basement where waitresses in green skirts were carrying green trays to different tables. A queue wound up the spiral staircase.

"Too many people," said Jeff. "We'd have to wait for hours. Let's go somewhere else."

Dawn and Lisa leant over the rail to look down into the restaurant. It was lit by green and orange lights. The people in the queue looked like aliens, each of them with half their face green and the other half orange. Dawn and Lisa looked at each other, wondering if their own faces looked as strange. There were plants everywhere, and just below the stairs was a shallow pool with a fountain in the middle.

"Oh, Daddy, look!" said Lisa. "It's got a fountain! Please let's stay! I don't think the queue will take very long."

"If they'd had any sense," said Jeff, "they'd have put an extra couple of tables there instead of that fountain, and cut the queue down a bit."

"Look, it's got a waterfall as well!" said Lisa. "This pool leads to another one over there. Oh, it looks so nice, with all those lovely leaves."

"They aren't real, you know," said Jeff. "Plastic, I should think."

Some people who had finished their meal came up the stairs, and Jeff pulled the two girls away from the rail. "Come on, you're getting in the way," he said. "We'll go and get a burger somewhere where there isn't such a queue."

They took a last look down at the pool with its sparkling fountain reflecting the green lights shining on it, and followed Jeff out into the street.

Chapter

≈ *11* ≈

"We need a picnic today," Lisa told Jeff at breakfast on Thursday. "We're going to the park with Poppy after swimming, and she's bringing a picnic, too."

"What do you need for a picnic, then?" asked Jeff. "I've got bread. You can make some sandwiches."

"Well," said Lisa. "A proper picnic would really have crisps and chocolate biscuits, and things like that."

"But sandwiches would do," said Dawn. "What shall we put in them?"

Jeff opened the fridge and looked inside.

"I wonder what this is?" he said, peering into a plastic carton. "It looks a bit old." He put it back on the shelf. "Ah, here's some cheese. Cheese sandwiches?"

"I don't like cheese," said Lisa. "I'll have jam."

"Not very nourishing," said Jeff. "You had better have some lettuce as well."

"It's not very fresh," said Lisa. The lettuce was so limp that it was hanging down over the edge of the fridge shelf.

"Well, an apple, then," said Jeff. "Make yourselves some sandwiches and I'll give you fifty pence for crisps or whatever else you want."

"Fifty pence each?" asked Lisa. Dawn nudged her and frowned.

"Fifty pence between you," said Jeff. "I don't want you stuffing yourselves with sweets, whatever you may be used to."

"We hardly ever eat sweets at home," said Dawn.

They packed up their lunch and squeezed it into their swimming bags.

"I'll see you some time this afternoon, then," said Jeff. "Have fun."

On the bus, Lisa said, "I can have a go in the canoe, can't I?"

"Poppy said that you couldn't until you had learnt to swim," said Dawn. "It wouldn't be safe. Maybe tomorrow you'll get your ten metres badge, and then we can arrange to go canoeing with her another time."

"I want to try it today," said Lisa. "I know I can swim ten metres if I try. I think I'm better on my back than my front."

"But the teacher won't be testing us today," said Dawn hopefully. "She'll just be teaching us today, and save the tests until the last lesson, tomorrow."

But Lisa was determined to have a turn in the canoe. When they had reached the pool, and changed into their swimming things, she went to find the teacher, who was getting her register and her whistle out of a cupboard.

Dawn watched. She wouldn't have dared to go and speak to the teacher, and anyway she didn't think the teacher would agree to change her plans.

But Lisa came bouncing back. "She says I can do it straight after the lesson ends! I told her that it was very urgent. Now I can get my badge and Poppy will let me try out the canoe."

"You might not manage it," Dawn reminded her. "This is only your fourth lesson."

"I don't know whether to practise extra hard during the lesson," said Lisa, "or rest as much as I can so that I'm not too tired to swim at the end of the lesson."

At the end of the lesson Dawn stood dripping on the edge of the deep pool to watch Lisa try for her ten metres.

"Did you want to try it today as well?" the teacher asked Dawn. She had not noticed that Dawn had not learnt to swim at all. Dawn shook her head.

"In you go, then, Lisa."

Lisa jumped in. "Just once across?" she asked.

"That not far enough for you?" the teacher asked. "Hurry up, I'm supposed to be teaching another class in a minute."

Lisa turned round, kicked up her legs and set off backwards across the pool. The only time she faltered was when she tried to wave at Dawn and give her a thumbs-up sign as she swam, and then she nearly sank. But she managed not to let her feet touch the bottom, and reached the other side safely.

"Fine," said the teacher, who had been filling in a

form while Lisa swam. "Give this to the person in the ticket kiosk, and they will give you your badge. Well done. We'll see if you can do your twenty-five metres tomorrow." She marched off.

"Was she joking?" Lisa asked. "Or do you think I really could swim twenty-five metres?"

"Of course you couldn't," said Dawn. "It's the whole length of the big pool. And it's deep at the other end, deeper than you. Don't you try it."

"I think she must have been joking," said Lisa.

Poppy was already dressed, waiting in the changing room. "Where have you two been?" she asked. "Everyone else came out ages ago."

Lisa waved her piece of paper. "I told you I would be able to swim by today," she said. "I've got my ten metres. Now I can try canoeing."

"That's very good," said Poppy. "Are you sure you never swam before this week? Oh, but I don't know about canoeing. Ten metres isn't very far. I mean, it is extremely good that you did it, but it doesn't mean that you are a really strong swimmer yet, and the river does pull you about quite a lot. I'm only supposed to use the canoe if Diane is there."

"Oh, it's all right," said Lisa. "The teacher said I could take my twenty-five metres tomorrow. I'm pretty good."

"She was only joking," said Dawn, squirming into her clothes. "You know she was. It probably isn't really safe for you to try the canoe. We can watch, and Poppy will show us how to do it."

"That's not fair!" said Lisa. "You said I could if I learnt to swim. You promised."

"Get dressed, anyway," said Poppy. "Maybe you can if I'm nearby to help if you get into difficulties."

"Don't let her drown," said Dawn. "Jeff would kill me."

Lisa dressed as quickly as she could. "I'm going to get my badge now," she said. She marched along to the ticket kiosk and proudly presented the piece of paper that her teacher had given her.

"You've taken a test already, have you?" said the woman in the kiosk. "They don't usually do them until tomorrow. Let's see, have I got a ten metres badge. Yes, here they are. That will be fifty pence."

"Oh," said Lisa. "Do I have to pay for it?"

"I'm afraid so," said the woman. "Fifty pence."

"Dawn!" called Lisa. "Give us that fifty pence that Dad gave us."

"What for?" asked Dawn. "They don't sell crisps here, do they?"

"No," said Lisa. "I need it for my badge. It's lucky, we've got just the right amount of money."

"It's not lucky," said Dawn. "Now we won't have any crisps."

Lisa paid for the badge and admired it. "I'll get Dad to sew it on my swimming costume tonight. There, Poppy. Proof!"

"I did believe you," said Poppy. "I just wasn't sure if you were good enough to try the canoe, that's all."

When they reached the weir, Diane and Jenny were already there, wearing swimming costumes and plimsolls. Diane was in the canoe and Jenny was watching from the bank. Dawn and Lisa hung back, and walked behind Poppy.

"We thought we'd better come down early to-day," they heard Diane say. "We found some kids messing about with the canoe yesterday."

"It wasn't kids messing about," said Poppy. "It was Dawn and Lisa. I asked them to empty the rain-water out, and you chased them away."

Diane looked at Dawn and Lisa. "Oh yes, it was you! Why didn't you say who you were?"

"You did scream at them," said Jenny.

"We didn't recognise you," said Diane. "I'm sorry. Are you going to have a go in the canoe?" She brought it close up to the bank and offered the paddle to Dawn.

Dawn took a step backwards. "I'd better not," she said. "I can't swim."

"I can," said Lisa. "Look, I got my ten metres badge today." She waved it at them.

"Do you think she would be all right if we stay close by her?" Poppy asked.

"She can't come to much harm with three of us to grab on to her," said Diane. "Get your swimming things on. Are you sure you don't want a go, Dawn? We wouldn't let you drown."

But Dawn had had enough of water for one day.

Poppy and Lisa went behind a tree and got into

their cold wet swimming costumes.

"Shall I put my trainers on?" asked Lisa.

"You'd better," said Poppy. "It's rough on the bottom. Stones, and maybe broken glass and stuff. People have picnics on the boats and chuck things in."

Dawn looked at Lisa's pink trainers that Mum had bought her for the holiday. They would not be pink after paddling in that dark water. Jenny's plimsolls were dark grey. Dawn went up on to the plank bridge and counted ducks while the others took turns in the canoe. Lisa nearly capsized, but the others held the canoe steady.

"I nearly did it on my own," she shouted to Dawn. "Watch me!"

Dawn watched, and then while the other girls had a turn in the canoe, she watched geese gliding along on the dark water and felt grateful that she was not a goose.

"Shall we show them what we do on the weir?" said Jenny.

Where the water of the weir came tumbling down the smooth concrete slope, waterweed had grown and made the slope slippery. Jenny and Diane climbed up the grass bank beside the weir, walked along at the top where the water was only ankle-deep and then sat down and slid with the water to the pool below. They gasped, splashed, and struck out for the shore again.

"I'm going to try it," said Poppy, and she climbed

up and slid down into the pool.

"I could do that," said Lisa.

"No, you couldn't," said Dawn.

"What about if two of us held her hands?" asked Diane. "Then we could make sure she came up again at the bottom."

Diane and Poppy sat on either side of Lisa at the top of the slope and slid down with her, heaving her up out of the water when they landed in the pool.

"That was wonderful," said Lisa. "You should try it, Dawn."

Then Diane tried sliding down on her feet, as though she were ski-ing down the slope. The first time she fell, but the second time she managed it.

"Let's try it with the canoe," said Poppy. "Shooting the rapids."

Using the rope that was tied to one end of the canoe, they pulled it along the upper part of the river until they were at the top of the weir. They stood on the plank bridge and eased the canoe through the rails until nothing but the rope was stopping the canoe from plunging down the weir to the pool below.

"Hold tight," said Poppy. "Let go when I say."

She climbed through the railing and lowered herself into the canoe, still holding on to the rail with one hand.

"Pass me the paddle," she said. Jenny handed it to her.

"All right!"

The rope was let go, and the canoe shot over the edge of the weir. Dawn was afraid it would carry straight on down into the pool, but as it hit the water at the bottom, the nose came up. The canoe swirled around for a moment in the churning water, and then Poppy managed to steer it back to the bank.

"It looks lovely," said Lisa. "Can't I try it, too?" But she knew that she couldn't. "Maybe when I get my twenty-five metres," she said.

"Or your fifty," said Poppy.

"You'd better not tell your father about this," said Diane. "We haven't told ours. I mean, he knows about the canoe, of course, but he thinks we just paddle around in the boring bits of the river."

"Jeff doesn't know about the canoe at all," said Dawn.

"Keep it that way," said Poppy.

On Friday the swimming lessons ended. Dawn had
to try for her ten metres badge, and this time the
teacher did notice that she had her feet on the bottom. But as soon as they left the sports centre, the
shame of being in a class with tiny children, and of
always being the last to jump in, and of being almost
the only one who ended up without a badge, floated
away. Dawn felt light and free. What made her feel
even better was that she had overheard a mother
saying that all the classes for the next week were
fully booked up. That meant that Jeff could not send
them back to learn any more swimming, even if he
had wanted to.

Poppy was going somewhere with her mother
today, so Dawn and Lisa planned to buy postcards
to send to Mum, and to look in the toy department
at Selfridges, and to see if the woman who sometimes drew chalk pictures on the pavement by the
Council offices was drawing anything there today.
First they went through the shopping centre. Lisa
flew along it upside-down on the ceiling.

"Be careful," said Dawn. "You don't look where
you're going. Can't you see in the mirror when there
are people coming towards you?"

"I don't crash into them very hard," said Lisa. "Anyway, they should be looking where they are going, too."

Dawn saw some computer games flashing on screens in a shop window. She went to watch. The games played themselves, and the computer always won. Suddenly there was a shout. Dawn knew that Lisa had bumped into someone. She turned and saw Lisa on hands and knees on the floor. There was another shout. Dawn looked harder, and saw that someone else was down on the floor. Pushing past a few shoppers, she rushed to Lisa's side.

"Are you all right?" she asked. "You idiot, I told you you should look where you were going. Did you knock the little boy over?"

The little boy was shouting. Dawn wished he would get up and go away. The fall could not have been that bad. She pulled Lisa to her feet.

"It's that little boy," said Lisa excitedly. "The one from the museum! He liked being crashed into!"

Dawn looked at the child. He was looking up at them with a delighted grin, and shouting again. His mother was beside him.

"That was great, wasn't it, Danny?" she said. "I suppose you couldn't manage it again, could you? Nothing that exciting generally happens to us here. People don't usually get down to Danny's level."

Dawn looked doubtfully at the woman. She could not actually be pleased that Lisa had tripped over her son?

"All right," said Lisa. "I'll do it again." She stepped right over the little boy, and pretended to fall to the ground. He shrieked with delight.

"Come on," said Dawn, embarrassed. "You can't do that here."

"What are your names?" asked the woman. "I'm Michelle, and this is Daniel."

Dawn never spoke to strangers. Lisa always did, but then she knew that Dawn was there to look after her.

"I'm Lisa," she said. "That's Dawn. Can't he walk?"

"No, he can't walk yet, but he's learning fast, and he can understand everything that you say."

Lisa was confused for a moment. "I'm sorry, Daniel," she said. "I didn't mean to be rude, talking about you. Do you like crawling about here?"

"We ought to go," said Dawn. She didn't know why the woman should want to talk to them. She didn't understand why the little boy had to crawl everywhere. Surely the woman could put him in a wheelchair and push him? He was probably small enough even to fit into an ordinary push-chair.

"We don't have to go," said Lisa stubbornly. "We haven't got to be back until lunch-time."

"I don't want to waste your time," said the woman, "but it's hard for Danny to get to know people. And it's good for him to meet new people, even if it's only for a few minutes, and specially people who are kind enough to fall over him and give him a good laugh."

"He didn't get hurt, did he?" asked Dawn.

"You didn't get hurt, did you, Dan?" said the woman. "No, he doesn't feel pain as much as he should. When he starts kicking up a big fuss about every bump and scratch, I'll know he's really improving. We'd better not stop work. Do you two have time to help for a few minutes? It would really encourage him if you could go ahead of him, so that he's got something to aim at. Go on, Danny, all the way to the end!"

Lisa walked backwards in front of the little boy. She crouched, to get as nearly down to his level as she could, and clapped her hands.

"Go on, Daniel!" she called. "Come and get me!" She walked backwards into a woman with two full carrier bags. Dawn hung back, not knowing what to do.

Daniel crawled the full length of the shopping centre, laughing and shouting. Sometimes Lisa nearly let him catch up with her, and then she would leap backwards out of his reach. His mother turned him round when he was almost at the huge glass doors that led out to the street, and he crawled all the way back again. He did it four times.

"You're a good boy!" said his mother, picking him up and hugging him. Dawn wondered if they could go now, and leave this strange woman and her poor child.

"Why does he have to crawl all the time?" Lisa

asked. "Is it to keep him fit?"

"It's to make him fit," said the woman. "His brain was hurt when he was born, and he has a lot of hard work to do to make it work properly again. He has to learn to crawl before he can walk. He has to learn a lot of other things, too, but he's getting there. He's a real fighter, aren't you, Dan?"

Daniel leaned back in his mother's arms and gave her a big crooked smile.

"He's got to learn to talk, hasn't he?" said Lisa. "And what about his eyes? Will they learn to go straight? Sometimes they seem to go off in different directions."

Dawn gasped. Lisa was so rude. She pulled at Lisa's sleeve.

"No," said Lisa, shaking Dawn off. "I want to know. I didn't know that handicapped people can get better. Maybe that funny old man that's always down by the canal at home could get better."

The woman didn't mind the questions, and Daniel didn't seem to mind either. "We're working on everything," she said. "He's improved a lot already. When he was a baby, the doctors said that he would never be able even to move about. His eyes were crossed all the time and didn't seem to see anything. He was deaf as well. They said he was a cabbage. But he isn't a cabbage at all. He's a very nice person, and I want him to be able to have a bit more fun. I want him to be able to sing songs and play football."

Dawn thought the woman was asking rather too

much. The woman guessed what she was thinking.

"I've met other children who've done it," she said. "Children who can run about now, who were just as bad as Daniel a few years ago. Danny does exercises for ten hours every day, and every day you can see the progress he's making."

"What sort of exercises?" Lisa asked.

Dawn stepped back. It was useless trying to get Lisa away. The woman didn't seem dangerous, but she was odd, and the child was odd too, and Dawn felt uncomfortable with them. She waited, and tried to look over towards the computer games again, but felt it would be rude to walk away.

"He has to crawl eight hundred metres each day," the woman was saying. "At first we just did it at home, but our house isn't big, and he got fed up going round and round the dining room and up and down the hall. So when we can, we come somewhere with a nice smooth floor to give ourselves a change. Of course, it's no good here on a Saturday. Too crowded."

"And sometimes you go to the museum," said Lisa. "We saw you there, but we didn't know what you were doing. What does he have to do as well as crawling?"

Dawn moved slowly over to the shop window, and watched a little green man walk across a screen collecting yellow blobs. When he reached the other side a grey square fell on his head, and then he reappeared back on the left of the screen, without

117

any yellow blobs. Dawn watched the same thing happen several times. She looked as well at her own reflection in the shop window, and felt dissatisfied with it. Her hair looked like flat snakes from being in the swimming pool, and she thought that her glasses made her look unfriendly. She tried smiling at herself, but it was only half a smile.

"Dawn!" called Lisa. "Come over here!"

Reluctantly Dawn joined the little group under the mirror. Daniel was bending back to look in the mirror above him, and laughing loudly. He did have a nice laugh. Dawn thought he seemed very cheerful for someone who had recently been a cabbage.

"We can help with Danny's exercises!" said Lisa, as though it was what she had been longing to do all her life. "Michelle needs people to help her with his exercises at home, and she says we can go and help if we like! Please can we, Dawn? Please?"

Dawn looked at the woman. The woman smiled back at her. "It's all right if you don't want to," she said. "But I could do with help, and there are lots of things that would be useful even if you aren't good at crawling. I need pictures cut out of magazines and stuck on cards so that Danny can look at them and learn their names. I need songs sung to him, and I need his feet tickled, and I could even do with someone making me a cup of tea sometimes when I'm busy with the exercises. I do have a lot of help from neighbours, but some of my helpers are students, and they're away on holiday at the moment, so we are short. But don't if you don't want to."

Dawn thought that a normal polite person would have seen that she did not want to help at all, and would have made it easy for her to refuse. This woman was not making it easy at all, and Dawn resented it. But then she thought that if the woman really needed help badly, and the little boy wouldn't get better without it, then it was fair enough for the woman to do everything she could to make people help her.

"We'll have to ask our father," said Dawn. "But I suppose I could stick pictures on card and make cups of tea. And maybe you could show me how to do other things, like exercises." She said it stiffly, and didn't want to say it at all. "Of course, we won't be in Oxford for very long. We could only come a few times."

"We aren't going home until the Saturday after next," said Lisa. "We could come every day until then."

"I would be very grateful for any help at all," said the woman. "We would both be very grateful. I think if you did come to help, you might enjoy it."

"We'd better write down your phone number," said Dawn. "Then if our father says it's all right for us to come, we'll ring you and you can tell us when you want us."

"I haven't got a pencil," said the woman, feeling in her pockets.

"Nor have we," said Dawn, half wishing that

having no pencil would mean the end of the arrangement. Of course it didn't.

"Hold Danny for a moment," said the woman, putting the boy into Dawn's arms. She ran into the shop with the computers. Dawn was terrified. The little handicapped boy must be so fragile. Supposing she dropped him? He laughed at her, and she had to smile back. Then his mother came out of the shop with a scrap of paper with her telephone number and address written on it. She took her son back from Dawn.

"There you are," she said. "Give me a ring this afternoon. We'll be at home. It would be great if you start tomorrow."

"We will ring," said Dawn. Perhaps Jeff would say that they couldn't go.

"That's terrific," said the woman. "Goodbye for now!"

"Goodbye!" shouted Lisa. "See you tomorrow!" Daniel gave a goodbye shout and nearly leapt out of his mother's arms; Dawn and Lisa went to buy a postcard for their mother.

'Dear Mum, This tower is the oldest building in Oxford. I hope you are well. Lisa is well and we are not forgetting to brush our teeth but we miss you. We have been to two museums. Love Dawn.'

'Dear Mum, I got my ten metres yesterday. We are going to teach a little boy to walk. One of Daddy's friends has a bike with one wheel. Love Lisa.'

Chapter

≈ *13* ≈

Dawn had a bath on Friday night and washed away the chemicals from the swimming pool. She could not fully enjoy the pleasure of having finished the swimming, because to enjoy it fully she would have to think about the awfulness of those lessons. She still couldn't bear to remind herself of them at all. She knew that later on she would have to go through it all in her mind, and try to turn it into something dull and distant, but at the moment it was still recent enough to sting. The embarrassment of pretending that her feet were not on the bottom, and of seeing the little children swimming first a few strokes, and then right across the pool, made a knot in her chest.

Dreading the swimming classes had made the last few days pass quickly. Each day there was the next lesson to think about. Suddenly Dawn realised that they had been away from home for a whole week, and it would still be another week before they saw Mum again. She was not quite homesick, but she did feel that it wouldn't be possible to relax properly until next Saturday came round and they were in the coach going home.

And now there was something new to face.

Jeff thought that it was a wonderful idea for Dawn and Lisa to help Michelle with her little handicapped boy. He rang her up himself from the downstairs telephone, to offer their services. Dawn thought that of course it was the sort of idea that a teacher would like. Teachers were always trying to encourage children to help in the community. Daniel was the bit of the community that needed help.

"I'll come down with you tomorrow," said Jeff. "I had better meet the woman. Maybe she doesn't really want to be lumbered with the two of you."

"She asked us to help," said Lisa indignantly. "Of course she wants us."

"Perhaps she was just being polite," said Dawn.

Lisa spoke to Michelle after Jeff. "She says Daniel is looking forward to seeing us," said Lisa.

"How does she know?" said Dawn. "He can't say so, can he?"

Jeff told the other people in the house that Lisa and Dawn were going to help look after a handicapped child. "I suppose you will be going most days, won't you?" he said at tea-time. They were eating a sort of vegetable stew that Sarah had cooked.

"He has to do exercises for ten hours every day," said Lisa. "I don't think we'll stay for ten hours every day, will we, Dawn?"

"We'll go for one hour tomorrow," said Dawn, firmly, "and see what it's like. Maybe we won't be any good at helping with the sort of exercises he has to do."

"What's wrong with the little boy?" said Sarah. "Oh, look, all the beans sank to the bottom. Would anyone like some extra beans?"

"There's not much wrong with him," said Lisa. "He looks quite intelligent really, except that his eyes don't always focus properly. And he can't walk or talk yet, but he is learning."

"Hmm," said Sarah. "It sounds as though he's got quite a long way to go. I wonder what sort of exercises he's supposed to do?"

"It's quite possible that he's just physically handicapped," said Jeff, "and that there's nothing wrong with his intelligence at all. He probably needs a lot of mental stimulation. Perhaps you should take some books to read to him."

"Or pictures to show him," suggested someone else. "I've got a lot of geography magazines in my room. They have some marvellous photographs in them, of different landscapes, people of different cultures and so on. Perhaps you'd like to borrow some of those to show him."

"Wasn't that a trumpet I saw up on your top shelf?" Lisa asked Sarah. "Could we borrow that? He might never have heard a trumpet before."

"Certainly," said Sarah. "You can borrow anything you like."

"I don't think we should take anything tomorrow," said Dawn. "We'll just go, and do whatever his mother wants us to do, and then we can see what sort of things he is interested in. He may be deaf, for all we know. And anyway, you don't know how to play a trumpet, Lisa."

"Very sensible, Dawn," said Jeff. "Good teaching practice. Observe first, identify problems and tasks second, implement last of all. Do you mind if I don't eat all of the beans, Sarah? It was a lovely stew, but I'm just a bit..."

"They were extremely tough, Sarah," said the pale quiet man who always sat reading at the end of the table. "I don't think you soaked them for long enough."

"I thought they were all right," said Sarah cheerfully, chewing hard.

"My turn to wash up," said Jeff. "You girls can help me. Clear away the plates, Lisa, and you can come and start drying, Dawn. I'll tell you where the things go."

"Where Michelle lives," Dawn asked, "is it far from here?"

"No," said Jeff. "It's this side of Oxford. You can walk down through the meadow."

Dawn thought about the meadow with the ponies and cows wandering over it, and the boats low down on the river which she had thought were creeping monsters. It seemed a very long time since the first time they had walked there. It was only a week ago.

"Have you got as much done as you planned?" she asked Jeff. "We've been here a whole week."

"Yes, I've done quite well," said Jeff. "I sent off

a whole batch of papers yesterday. I did wonder whether I would be able to get any work done at all while you were here. You were quite – quite demanding when you were younger."

"So we haven't been getting in your way?"

"No," said Jeff, sounding a little surprised. "No, I suppose not. I must say, I was rather nervous about having you to stay down here. But it seems to be working out all right. I shan't worry so much next time you come."

So he was expecting them to come another time. Dawn was relieved. She had felt that she and Lisa were on trial, and that if Jeff decided that they were not interesting enough, or not well enough behaved, he might go back to just writing them letters twice a year. Of course, he hadn't said how often he'd want to see them, but then she wasn't sure herself how often she'd want to come. It was much too far to come every weekend. At least he wanted to go on being their father.

"Go on, Jeff," said Sarah. She had come into the kitchen and was scraping the remains of her vegetable stew into the bin. "It's a nice change for you, isn't it, having them here? He gets bored up there all on his own, Dawn. He's normally hanging round the television saying what nonsense all the programmes are, or eating our biscuits, even though he's got a perfectly good supply of his own upstairs. It's great to see him getting out with you two sometimes."

"Where do you keep the biscuits, then, Daddy?" asked Lisa. "I haven't seen any."

"You should have kept that stew, Sarah," said Jeff. "It was all right. Somebody would have eaten it up."

"I don't know who," said Sarah. "Here, wash the saucepan out, and stop trying to change the subject."

The house where Michelle and little Daniel lived was close to the meadow, but nearer to the town centre than Jeff's house. It was a tiny house in the middle of a row of tiny houses. The houses on either side had brightly-painted doors and windows, and window-boxes on the sills full of pink and red and orange flowers. Michelle's front door was peeling.

"It looks a bit shabby, doesn't it?" said Lisa, wrinkling her nose. "I wish they lived in that house with the nice flower basket over the front door."

"She's probably too busy with the little boy to bother with making it look smart," said Dawn. "Anyway, I expect those flower baskets drip all over the front step when they water them."

Jeff knocked on the door. It was opened by an old woman in an apron.

"Oh, I wonder if we've come to the wrong house?" said Jeff. "Number twenty-three, isn't it?"

"That's right," said the old woman. "Michelle's expecting you. I'm one of her helpers, but I'm just leaving. Come on in."

Dawn thought that if Michelle already had people helping her, she wouldn't really need them as well. She followed Lisa and Jeff into the dark little entrance hall as the old woman took off her apron and let herself out at the front door.

Jeff crashed into something. "What on earth?" he said, rubbing his side.

There was a sort of ladder fixed against the wall, level with Dawn's chest. It was not flat against the wall, but was fixed on brackets so that the rungs were horizontal. It took up half the hall, which was narrow enough anyway. Dawn could see that another ladder led into a room at the back of the house. They had to duck under the ladder to get into the front room. Dawn saw Jeff frowning, and wondered whether he would think that this house was too weird for them to visit on their own.

In the front room, Daniel was being rolled about on the floor. Michelle was kneeling on one side of him, and another woman on the other side, and they were rolling the little boy to each other across the carpet.

Jeff cleared his throat. He probably expected Michelle to jump to her feet and shake his hand.

"Hello," said Michelle, without looking up. "I'm glad you've come. I'll be with you in a minute. Two more minutes of this. It's to help with Daniel's balance."

Daniel rolled to and fro, to and fro, and Dawn wondered how it could possibly help with his balance. Jeff stood with his hands in his pockets looking out of the window, as though it wouldn't be polite to watch Daniel being rolled. Lisa was looking at the heap of papers on the table under the window.

"Look, Dawn," she said. "Dinosaurs. Bats. Planets." She held up a piece of card which had pictures of different kinds of bats stuck on it.

"Lisa!" said Jeff.

"It's all right," said Michelle. "Have a look round. One more minute. Your visitors are here, Danny. We'll just finish this, and you can show them how you walk."

"Does this really help him?" Jeff asked. "I mean, I've never heard of this kind of treatment. It does seem rather unconventional. What good can it do the child?"

Michelle didn't answer. Dawn thought it was because she had got into the rhythm of rolling Daniel to and fro, to and fro, and didn't want to break it, but she knew that Jeff might think it rudeness. Suddenly a bell went off, shrill and continuous like an alarm clock. Michelle sat back on her heels and picked up a kitchen timer that was next to her on the floor. She switched it off.

Daniel pulled himself to his knees and set off, crawling, to the door. Michelle lifted him on to his feet and placed his hands on the rungs of the ladder. Then Dawn saw what it was for. When he was holding on to the ladder, he could walk. It was like having a grown-up's hand on each side of him to hold on to and to help him walk, except that the rungs were right above his head, and stretching up to hold them he looked straight and tall. He walked along to the end of the hall, then switched to the other ladder and disappeared into the other room.

"He likes showing off to new people," said Michelle. "Yes, thanks, Mrs Pratley, I'll see you on Monday. 'Bye!"

The other woman left.

"Could you explain a little about what you want my daughters to do for you?" said Jeff, still frowning.

"Oh, yes," said Michelle. "I expect they'll have a lot of questions to ask. I'll try and answer as we go along."

"But what is all this?" Jeff asked. "Do you really think that rolling the child around on the carpet is going to make him walk?"

Michelle took a deep breath, as though she might explain everything, then shrugged her shoulders. "Yes," she said. "I do. You see, an awful lot of people write off children like Daniel. They think that they will never walk, maybe never even talk. I could send him to a special school every day, and they would do their best for him there. He'd probably learn some things that I couldn't teach him, but they wouldn't be working at re-wiring his brain. I think that's the first thing that needs doing, so that's what we're working at. The trouble is, this method isn't officially recognised in this country. I have to rely on jumble sales to pay for the equipment, and volunteers to give up an hour or two every week to help

130
~

work on Dan. There isn't time now to explain how I know this is the right thing to be doing. But I do know, I promise." Then she called out, "Danny! Come back here! I've got a biscuit for you!"

Daniel reappeared, grinning, and swung his way back along the ladder, hand over hand, his thin legs moving along underneath. He slid down to the ground and took the biscuit.

"We have to spin him round now," said Michelle. "Could you help me get him into the chair, Dawn? I can do it on my own, but it's easier with two."

The chair was the sort of office chair that spins round on one central leg. Daniel sat on it and was held securely on to it by a sort of harness. Two bath sponges fixed to the chair-back held his head upright. Dawn had noticed that his neck was weak and his head usually tipped to one side. It gave him a rather nice look, she thought, as though he was always asking questions, or considering things.

"Set the timer for three minutes, Lisa, please," said Michelle.

"But he's only just eaten," said Jeff. "He'll be sick."

"Why don't you go home now," said Michelle, "and the girls can tell you all about it later?"

Jeff waited for a minute or two, watching uncomfortably as Michelle spun Daniel round on the chair.

Then he said, "I suppose I had better go and get some work done. See you later."

"What work does your father do?" Michelle

asked, as she spun the chair round a few times in one direction, and then stopped it and spun it the other way round.

"He marks exam papers," said Dawn. "He's a teacher really. The exam papers are just to earn extra money in the holidays."

"There isn't really time to explain the whole thing to someone all at once," said Michelle. "It's easier to explain things to people as we go along."

"What is this for?" said Lisa. "How will this help Daniel to walk?"

Michelle stopped the chair again and spun it in the opposite direction. "He can walk under the ladders," she said, "as you see. He's got the right movements, but his balance isn't good. I want him walking on his own, but there isn't a chance of that until he knows more about which way up he is, and how the different bits of him join on to each other. Spinning him gives him loads of practice at wondering which way round he is."

When the timer went off, Daniel looked quite dazed. He leaned against Michelle when she unstrapped him, with his eyes closed.

"What are we supposed to do?" asked Lisa. "Can I spin him round?"

"That's all the spinning for now," said Michelle. "But we do it fifteen times a day, so you can help again later. Come on, Danny, crawling time now."

She put him down gently on the floor, where he lay, smiling crookedly up at her.

"Come on, Dan, crawl to the kitchen door and back here, and you can have a raisin."

Daniel set off. Lisa walked behind him.

"Does he have to do things all day?" asked Dawn. "Doesn't he get tired out?"

"He does get tired," agreed Michelle. "And he doesn't always feel like working. But anything's better than having to sit in a wheelchair for the rest of your life. A couple of years ago I thought he would never crawl. Then he learned to stand up holding on to the ladder, but he couldn't move along it. He's going to walk on his own, one of these days."

Daniel crawled back into the room and took his raisin.

"He went right to the back door," Lisa reported. "I told him to touch it."

"That's good," said Michelle. "He'll have to do that five more times." Daniel said something that sounded like, "No."

"Yes, you will," said Michelle. "That's the main problem, you see. He gets bored, crawling up and down all the time. I was hoping you could help to make it more fun for him. He likes having stories read to him while he crawls, and we do his reading practice and his general knowledge at the same time, too."

"Reading?" said Dawn. "Can he read?"

Michelle showed her a pile of cards. Each one had a word printed on it.

"I'll do it," said Lisa, seizing the cards. "Come on,

Danny, what does this say?" She waved one of the cards at him.

"Well, he can't say the words all that well," said Michelle. "And he does actually know that particular one pretty well."

"Oh, all right," said Lisa. "I'll just keep him crawling, and you two can do the reading practice."

She crawled a little ahead of Daniel, and said, "I'll sing you a rude song when you've gone all the way to the kitchen and back."

"Lisa!" said Dawn, shocked. "Sing him something educational, like *Ten green bottles*."

Lisa sang *Ten green bottles* with rude variations and Daniel shrieked with delight.

"I'm good at this," said Lisa. "Can we come all day tomorrow?"

"You know we can't," said Dawn. "It's Jeff's turn to cook a big Sunday dinner for everyone in the house. We'll have to be there."

"Well," said Lisa. "We'll come in the morning, and then if Daddy doesn't want us for anything, we can come back in the afternoon."

"I thought I might take Dan to the Natural History Museum tomorrow afternoon," said Michelle. "It's a perfectly good floor for crawling, and he loves all the stuffed animals."

"Oh, we've been to that one," said Lisa. "Do you remember, Dawn? The first day we went to the park, before we knew about the weir."

"Well, you'll know where to meet me if you

come in the afternoon, then," said Michelle. "Can you take him for another crawl, Lisa?"

Lisa and Daniel disappeared again and Dawn heard them giggling in the kitchen.

"Look, Dawn," said Michelle. "Here's something you can help with. I show Daniel pictures while he's working – sets of pictures, like ten pictures of the moon, or ten different sorts of motorbikes. You see, normal children learn all kinds of things, just by happening to be around when interesting things happen, or when grown-ups are talking about them. And of course they find out a lot by crawling around exploring. Daniel has missed out on several years of that, because of his eyes and his ears not working properly, and being uncomfortable so that he could not concentrate on anything outside himself. So now I'm trying to feed as much information into him as I can, so that he'll catch up. If you could go through these magazines and sort out the pictures, it would be really useful."

Dawn paged through the magazines, scissors in hand. She found some different chairs. Then she found a picture of someone making a chair, weaving its cane seat, and she made a collection of people making things: a builder, a violin maker and a car assembly worker.

"Shall I glue them on to the cards?" she asked. But Michelle had gone, and when Dawn listened, she could hear her in another room urging Daniel to walk under the ladder. So Dawn found some glue and stuck the pictures on to the cards. Then she went on searching. Ten machines, ten soldiers, ten kinds of electric light.

When it was time for Daniel to be rolled on the floor again, the girls helped, both of them on one side and Michelle on the other. When he had to be spun on the chair, Lisa had a go at spinning him.

"Watch out!" said Michelle. "That's a bit fast! Perhaps you'd better let Dawn have a go at it."

So Lisa went and sorted out toys that might encourage Daniel to crawl from end to end of the house, while Dawn carefully spun the little boy three times round to the left, three times round to the right. She was feeling giddy herself from watching, when the timer went off to tell them to stop. She wondered how Daniel felt. She undid his straps and he leant against her with his eyes closed. She looked down at his fine brown hair spread out against the grey wool of her cardigan. He was quite relaxed. She felt very proud, suddenly, that he trusted her enough to lean against her, and that Michelle trusted her enough to let her spin the frail child round and round until he was dizzy. It did seem a strange way of making him better, but Dawn could think of no reason not to believe that it was the right thing to be doing.

Jeff cooked a meat pie for Sunday dinner. The pastry was rather thick and Lisa thought the meat was chewy. All the grown-ups were very polite and encouraging about it. Dawn suspected that Jeff might have cooked worse things for them in the past. There was apple crumble for pudding.

"This crumble is interesting," said the pale man.

"It's lovely," said Sarah. "What did you put in it? It's got quite an unusual flavour."

"Flour and marge," said Jeff. "That's what crumble is made of, isn't it?"

"Well, I think it usually has a bit of sugar in," said Sarah. "But I suppose it doesn't have to."

"Sugar's bad for you," said Jeff. "I thought I would flavour it with a bit of pepper and some of that stuff on the top shelf."

"Oh, not Simon's spices!" said the pale man. "I thought it tasted odd."

The telephone rang while they were eating. Jeff was still feeling busy and efficient, from having cooked the dinner, so he ran to answer it.

"It was Dave," he said when he came back. "You know my friend with the three little girls that we met at the top of that tower?"

"Yes, Diane and Jenny's father," said Lisa.

"He was asking if you two would like to go swimming with them this afternoon. I think they are going to the Cowley swimming pool."

"Oh yes!" said Lisa. "Poppy was telling me about it! It's got two swimming pools and a really deep pool for diving into, with a big high board you can jump off. Poppy says she can jump backwards off it. I'm going to try!"

"You can't," said Dawn. "We said we would meet Michelle and Daniel at the museum this afternoon. They'll be expecting us."

Lisa looked horrified. "I can't miss the chance of going swimming," she said.

"I've already said that you would go," said Jeff. "You'll have to give your little boy a miss for this afternoon. The woman can't complain, after all. You did spend most of the morning there."

"But we promised," said Dawn. She was not sure herself which was the stronger feeling, that they shouldn't let Michelle and Daniel down, or that she couldn't bear to go swimming. Then she decided that not wanting to go swimming was an extremely strong feeling.

"I don't want to go swimming," she said. "And Poppy is more friends with Lisa than with me, anyway."

"Diane and Jenny will be there, too," said Lisa. "Poppy told me that she and her mother spend the weekends with Dave, and they go back to their own house during the week."

"Yes, you would like Diane," said Jeff. "And I thought you quite liked swimming. You enjoyed the lessons, didn't you?"

Dawn remembered Jeff had paid for the lessons, and had perhaps thought of them as a sort of holiday treat. "Well, I would rather not go swimming today," she said.

"I'll go swimming," said Lisa, "and Dawn can go and help with Daniel. That will be all right, won't it, Daddy?"

"I suppose so," said Jeff. "Dave said he would come and pick you up at about three. You'll have to explain about Dawn."

"Are you showing the little boy round the museum?" Sarah asked. "That should be nice for him."

"I think he'll be crawling most of the time," said Dawn. "He just gets to see the museum things as a reward when he's crawled far enough. He has to crawl for miles every day, and it's more interesting for him to go somewhere big like a museum."

"It sounds extraordinary," said Sarah.

Jeff shook his head. "That poor child," he said. "I think the woman is the one who's mad. She has her house full of ladders, and she spins him round and round on a swivelling chair. She's the one that's got something wrong with her, if you ask me."

"You don't know anything about it," said Dawn indignantly. "Neither of them is mad. Daniel is just handicapped, that's all. Bits of his brain don't send the right messages to the rest of his body. But it's better to try and help him get better, isn't it, than just letting him sit in a wheelchair for the rest of his life?"

Jeff looked a little ashamed. "Well, maybe it is worth trying," he agreed. "Good for you, if you want to help. I don't know anything about that sort of thing."

Dawn thought it was the first time she had contradicted her father. It was also the first time she had heard him say that he didn't know about something. "I don't know much about it yet, either," she said kindly. "I'll try and explain it to you when I find out more about it."

"Daddy," said Lisa. "Please will you sew my ten metres badge on my swimming costume before three o'clock? Poppy's got three badges on hers, and Diane has got a hundred metres badge."

"Diane?" said Jeff. "How do you know what badges she has got?"

"We happened to meet them in the University Parks," said Dawn.

"Oh, I remember now," said Jeff. "They've got a boat of some sort down there, haven't they?"

"A canoe," said Lisa. "It's brilliant."

Dawn gave her a warning look.

"Well, I suppose they're safe enough with a boat if they can swim as well as that," said Jeff. "But I wouldn't like to leave children of mine alone with a boat. You never know what may happen. Now listen, you two. If they ever suggest that you go in that boat with them, I want you to refuse. Understood?''

Lisa and Dawn nodded. Lisa made a crooked face and Jeff gave her a firm look to make sure she understood.

They went up to the attic and left Gordon to do the washing up. It was his turn. Dawn thought it was more friendly to do the dishes the way they did them at home, where things piled up until there were no clean dishes left at all, and then everyone helped to do them together. Jeff got out his blue cotton.

"It doesn't really match the costume," said Lisa. "Never mind, it will do. It blends in quite nicely with the badge. Do you think it would look better on the left or the right? Poppy put her first one quite near the bottom, on the left.''

Jeff put the badge in place and threaded his needle.

"No, I mean it was on the left from where I looked at it," said Lisa. "The other side.''

Jeff moved the badge over to the other side and put a knot at the end of the thread, pressing his lips tightly together.

"But I like it better the way you had it before," said Lisa. "Put it a little bit higher up, or it'll be sort of in the shadow of my fat tummy.''

Dawn watched as Jeff silently put the badge

where Lisa wanted it and began to sew it on. She didn't like his silence. It would have been more reasonable for him to throw the badge on the floor and tell Lisa to sew it on herself. Somehow, because he didn't complain, Dawn felt that he'd given up on them, and was thinking of them just as tiresome nuisances who would be gone in another week.

She waited a while, but Jeff's mouth stayed fixed in a straight, hard line. "You don't have to put up with her, you know," Dawn told him. "Always changing her mind. You should try and make her more polite."

"I wasn't rude," said Lisa. "I said 'please' when I asked him to sew it on, didn't I, Daddy? And I'll probably say 'thank you' when he's finished."

"You'd better," said Jeff, and he smiled. He looked up at Dawn. "You needn't worry," he said. "She's quite nice the way she is. And so are you. Really, I am pleased that you have both turned into such nice people. You were only babies before I went to Australia."

He had said it too quietly for Dawn to feel very pleased about it. This would have been the right time for him to hug them, and perhaps ask her to start calling him 'Dad' instead of 'Jeff'. Instead, he went on sewing round the edge of the badge and Lisa went to fetch her towel.

It was time for Dawn to set off for the museum, but she waited to see whether Jeff wanted to be friendly again before she left.

"You'd better be going, hadn't you?" he said. "I told Dave to bring the kids back for a cup of tea after they've been swimming, so try and get back by about five. I suppose I'd better go and buy some biscuits or something. I wonder if there are any shops open on a Sunday afternoon?"

Dawn left him wondering. She went down to the road and waited for the bus. Overhead, aeroplanes had left soft white trails in the sky. Dawn breathed in deeply and was delighted that she was not going swimming. She would probably never have to go swimming again. The sun warmed her back and the cars that drove by looked as bright as toys. She wondered whether she could have said politely, last week, that she didn't want to go to the swimming lessons. Today it had been so easy to say that she wouldn't go.

The bus came, shining red. The driver looked friendlier than usual. Perhaps he was near the end of his shift. He set off at high speed as soon as Dawn had paid for her ticket, and she swung her way happily along to the back seat, hanging on to the silver bars on either side. This would have been a good day for cycling. It was a day for moving fast through the air and tiring yourself out. Riding a unicycle would have suited the day, sitting up straight and tall on the saddle, arms folded, and grinning triumphantly at everyone you passed.

When the bus pulled up at the stop nearest to the museum, Dawn jumped off.

When Daniel caught sight of her, his crawling doubled speed. He raced towards her.

"I'm glad you came," said Michelle. "Danny's been looking for you round every corner."

"I'm sorry Lisa isn't here," said Dawn. "She had to go swimming with some friends. My father arranged it before he'd asked us."

Daniel sat back on his feet and laughed up at Dawn.

"Come on then, young man," said Michelle. "Show Dawn the way to the dinosaur skeletons."

But Daniel just sat and laughed.

"Here, I'll race you," said Dawn. She got down and began to crawl beside Daniel. He enjoyed this. Dawn found that it was hard on the knees, and her arms soon grew tired. She noticed a few people staring, but she pretended that they were staring because she was doing something rare and brilliant, like riding a unicycle, instead of crawling around a museum with a small boy.

"I don't know how he does it," she said to Michelle when they reached the dinosaurs. "I'm worn out, and he has to go a lot further than that."

"We'll have to find something else to lure him on," said Michelle. "I wonder what's in those cases over there?"

"Lovely crystals," said Dawn. "I saw them last time I was here. Come on, Danny, I'll show you some beautiful sparkly crystals." Daniel crawled to see the crystals, and then Dawn had to crawl beside him again to encourage him along the next stretch.

"What we need," said Michelle, "is a well-trained kitten that will go along in front of him, playing with a ping-pong ball at the same time and keeping just out of reach, to keep him going."

Dawn invented in her head a machine that would move along, doing interesting things to tempt Daniel forward. Then she realised that it had already been invented. "We've got one!" she said. "At least, I can borrow one."

"What! A kitten that goes two hundred yards at a stretch, playing with a ping-pong ball and never stopping?"

"Almost," said Dawn. "I'll see if I can bring it tomorrow."

Chapter

≈ *16* ≈

"I'm going down to see Sarah," Dawn said at breakfast on Monday. "I want to borrow some of her clockwork toys for Daniel."

"Does Sarah have clockwork toys?" said Jeff. "She is a strange person."

"She's got a tin whale that swallows a little fish," said Lisa. "You don't have to wind it up. You just pull the fish out of its mouth on a string, and that sets it off."

Jeff shook his head. "I don't understand grown adults who play with toys."

"I think she may just collect them," said Dawn. "But anyway, I thought it would encourage Daniel to crawl, if one of the toys was going along just ahead of him. It would give him something to watch. You could be in charge of winding them up, Lisa. You'd have to make sure they were far enough away for him not to catch them too easily."

"Oh, I can't go today," said Lisa.

"Can't go to see Daniel?" said Dawn. "Why not?"

"Now, come on, Lisa," said Jeff. "I know it was me that arranged that swimming outing yesterday, so that you couldn't go. But you did say you would be going every day. I don't think you can let the woman down like that. You can't start something and then just drop it for no reason."

"I haven't dropped it," said Lisa. She spoke crossly, so Dawn knew that she was feeling guilty at not wanting to go to Daniel's today. "It's just that I promised Poppy I would meet her by the weir in the park. We're taking our swimming costumes. And I promised Poppy, so I can't break my promise. She gets lonely when Diane and Jenny aren't there."

"You just as good as promised Michelle," said Dawn. "Talking about going there ten hours a day." But she felt really that it was fair enough for Lisa to want to spend time with her new friend. It was lucky that she had Daniel to keep her busy, and didn't have to tag along with the younger girls. She would probably make friends herself in Oxford one day, if they came here often. Diane looked quite nice. Then she would have to share out her time between little Daniel and her friends. For this week she didn't really mind if Lisa went off with Poppy.

"No, don't worry about it," she said. "Michelle won't mind, as long as one of us goes, and it would be a shame not to have fun with Poppy while you've got the chance. But I think you should come once or twice more before we go home, so that Daniel doesn't think you've forgotten him."

"I'll come tomorrow," said Lisa. "Maybe Poppy will come, too."

Jeff was more worried now about the weir. "The water may be deep," he said. "You can only swim ten metres, and that isn't enough to get you out of trouble. There may be quite a strong current."

"Poppy's a good swimmer," said Lisa. "She could rescue me."

"Poppy's hardly bigger than you are," said Jeff. "You'll probably both drown. No, I don't like the sound of this."

Dawn left them discussing the safety of swimming in the weir, and went down to see Sarah.

"Yes, of course!" said Sarah, when Dawn had explained what she wanted. She looked along the crowded shelves and found the toys that would be the most use. The little tin bird was nice, but it hopped round in circles, so that was no good.

"I know," said Sarah. "I've got a little circus truck somewhere. I wonder where I put it? It's not as good as these, really, because it has batteries. I like the clockwork ones best. But it will keep going right across a room. Maybe across a museum, I don't know."

She found the truck. When it was switched on, it crossed the floor steadily, and a sea-lion on the roof turned slowly round, balancing a metal ball on its nose, while a monkey waved its hand from side to side out of the rear window. The clown driving the truck turned his smiling face to left and right, but Daniel wouldn't be able to see that from behind.

"That looks great," said Dawn. "I'm sure he'll like it. I wouldn't mind crawling a mile or two watching that."

"Take the others as well," said Sarah. "Then he can have a bit of variety. And tell his mother she can keep them as long as she likes, if they do turn out to be useful. I won't miss them."

Michelle was delighted with the toys. Daniel crawled faster than ever. In fact he crawled too fast for the circus truck, and caught up with it, so they used it as a reward instead, and let him watch it cross the room once each time he had completed a crawling circuit.

"Those toys were a brilliant idea," Michelle said on Wednesday. "He's going further every day. It's so lucky I met you. You know, the man from the butcher's rang this morning to say that he can't come in this week because they are short-staffed. It would have been a disaster if you hadn't been here this week. And it's been fantastic for Daniel to see so much of you. He knows all the other helpers, of course, but they only come for an hour or so at a time, and then they disappear again. He's had time to get to know you properly, and he's got fond of you. It's nice."

On Thursday Daniel managed to catch up with the flashing robot, which was the fastest of all the toys, and gave it a triumphant bang on the floor, which stopped it flashing.

"Sarah won't mind," said Dawn. "I told her this morning how it was helping Daniel with his crawling, and she was really pleased."

When other people arrived to help with Daniel,

Dawn cut out more pictures.

"What set are you making now?" Michelle asked.

"Moving water," said Dawn. "I did a set of the sea, and now this is things like fountains and waterfalls. Look, here's a gargoyle with water gushing out of its mouth."

"We could show Danny one like that," said Michelle. "I must remember to look out for gushing gargoyles next time we are in town on a rainy day. But I'm afraid I won't be able to find a waterfall for him in Oxford. Just as well you've found some pictures to show him. It's amazing how many things he doesn't know about, once you start thinking about it."

"Oh, I know some waterfalls he could see in Oxford," said Dawn. "Lisa went to swim in one of them on Monday. At least, she wanted to, but Jeff said she mustn't. They may have gone there again today. It's a weir, really."

"Of course!" said Michelle. "There's a weir in the University Parks, isn't there? I'd forgotten all about it. Yes, that will do nicely as a waterfall. We must go there some time."

"Let's go there this morning," said Dawn. "After he's done his ladder-walking. Couldn't we? We might see Diane and Jenny canoeing down the weir. I think they go there quite often."

Michelle looked doubtful. "We have to fit in four more sessions of rolling and spinning before lunch," she said. "But Mrs Davis rang to say that her sister is ill, so she can't come in today. You know, this week everyone seems to be ill or away on holiday. If we can't stick to the routine, we may as well make the most of it. We can squeeze in an outing, if we get working. What do you think, Danny? Do you want to do some of your crawling at the University Parks?''

"Can he manage it on grass?" Dawn asked. "It's quite tufty in places, and there were molehills. Maybe he could crawl on the tennis courts. They looked nice short grass."

"Molehills would give him very useful practice in getting over obstacles," said Michelle. "Come on, Dan, back here and we'll give you a quick roll before we set off. We're going to see a waterfall!"

"Shall I show him the water pictures?" Dawn asked. "So that he knows what he's going to see?"

"We'll show him on the way," said Michelle. "Set the timer for three minutes, will you?"

Dawn brought all the water pictures with her and, by the time they reached the park, Daniel knew all about streams, rivers, lakes, oceans and waterfalls.

"Crawling first," said Michelle. "Show us this tennis court."

"You could probably come and crawl in my father's garden some time," said Dawn. "It's big, and the lawns are quite nice and smooth. There's a sort of front lawn and a back lawn. They're big. When he can walk, you could come by the path through the meadow. It goes almost all the way from our house to yours."

Nobody was playing tennis. Daniel crawled from end to end of the smooth grassy court eight times. Dawn crawled beside him until her arms wore out, and then ran backwards in front of him, cheering him on. It was just as tiring to run backwards. Her neck ached from looking round to see if the way was clear, and her back ached from bending down.

"I think you've earned a waterfall, Dan," said Michelle. "One more roll, and we'll go and find it. We'll have to count to sixty-three times, Dawn. I didn't bring the timer."

They rolled Daniel to and fro between them in the grass. Dawn thought that it must be much nicer for him to see the blue sky swinging giddily about overhead, than a dull ceiling at home.

"He ought to be able to walk in this weather," she said. "I feel like running when it's like this, and it seems so unfair that Danny can't run."

"I know," said Michelle. "It makes it all the easier to put up with ladders everywhere and the timer pinging all through the day. Maybe next summer he'll be able to get across the park on his own two feet. Sometimes I dream that he's walking towards me across a grassy field, a bit like this one. It's not too disappointing when I wake up, because I believe he will get there in the end."

They carried Daniel, limp and dizzy, along the path to the weir. Above the sound of rushing water they could hear excited voices.

"That's probably Lisa and Poppy," said Dawn. "I wonder if Jeff said they could swim after all? Or maybe he said they couldn't but they did anyway."

They came round the corner by the weir. Daniel sat up in Michelle's arms, listening to the strange noises.

"It's Dawn and Daniel!" shouted Lisa. "Look, Poppy, here's Daniel!"

"Did Jeff say you could swim?" said Dawn. The two girls were wearing their swimming costumes.

"No," said Lisa. "We're just sun-bathing."

"You look quite wet if you've only been sun-bathing," said Dawn.

"The sun's so hot," said Poppy. "Sometimes we have to cool ourselves down with a little bit of water. But we haven't actually been swimming. Mummy didn't want me to either, without Diane here."

Michelle was showing Daniel the weir. She carried him along the plank bridge that ran across the top of the weir. Daniel leant over the rushing water and shouted at it.

"He wants to get in!" called Michelle.

"We'll take him for a paddle," said Lisa. "Bring him down to the bottom where it's shallow. Poppy and I can hold him."

Michelle came back to the edge of the pool below the weir. "I've got nothing to dry him on afterwards," she said. "And he does get cold easily, even on a warm day like this."

"We've got towels," said Poppy. "We brought them just in case we got splashed or anything. Go on, let him have a paddle."

In the end they just rolled up Daniel's trousers and dangled his feet in the water. He kicked, and made everyone wet, and then screamed with laughter. Dawn stood back, out of reach of the splashes, but he reached out to her, wanting her to join in the fun. She took off her own socks and shoes and took him from Michelle, dipping his legs into the water and then swinging him so that silver drops of water flew off him into the sky.

"Do you know?" said Michelle. "About two years ago I took Danny swimming because I thought it might be good for him, and he screamed so much that I never went again. But I think he would like it now. What do you reckon, Dan? Would you like to go to a nice warm swimming pool, and get right in the water?"

Dawn thought of the smell, and the bare tiles, but she supposed that Daniel might not mind. She thought that Lisa and Poppy would probably love to help with him in the swimming pool.

"It would make a change for him, wouldn't it?" said Dawn.

"Yes," said Lisa. "It would be a lot more fun than all that crawling and rolling and stuff."

"I think it's definitely worth a try," said Michelle. "But we'll still have to keep on with the crawling. Would you fancy coming to help, then?"

She looked around at the three girls. Lisa was eager. Poppy was cautious, because she had still not worked out what sort of a person Daniel was. Dawn felt a little jealous of Lisa, who could offer to give Daniel this lovely treat of bathing in a swimming pool, and she felt ashamed that she could not offer to help herself.

"I wouldn't mind coming," said Poppy. "They have arm-bands you can borrow at the Ferry Pool. He could bob about with them on. If he can crawl, then I expect he could swim as well. You only have to sort of crawl with your legs, don't you, and that pushes you along in the water."

"I'll come," said Lisa. "I love swimming."

"You won't really need me if you've got the others to help," said Dawn.

"It would be nice if you came," said Michelle. "Daniel is bound to think it's all a bit strange, but he trusts you, and he might just find it easier with you there. What about tomorrow morning? We can meet you at the pool. Say eleven o'clock, then we'll have time to do our first lot of walking and crawling before we come. I'll have to find some underpants that are smart enough for you to swim in, Danny."

"Oh, tomorrow morning!" said Poppy. "Don't you remember, Lisa? We were meant to ask Dawn! My mum wants to take us all out for a picnic somewhere. She's got a day off work, and I was meant to be asking you as well, Dawn. She said she'd like to meet you both."

"It's our last day tomorrow," said Dawn. She imagined a picnic with Poppy's mother. Then she thought about the swimming pool.

"Of course you must go for your picnic," said Michelle. "Don't worry about the swimming. Maybe we can go next time you are in Oxford. It really doesn't matter a bit."

Dawn looked at Daniel, waving and shouting at the splashing weir, longing to be in it.

"I'll come swimming with you," she said. "Can you explain to your mother, Poppy? Say thank you for me, and all that. I would like to meet her, but Michelle's short of helpers this week, and Daniel may not get another chance of going swimming for ages."

"Do you think I should come, too?" asked Lisa. "You don't like swimming very much, do you?"

"It's all right," said Dawn. "Poppy's mother will be disappointed if she takes the day off and neither of us turns up. I don't mind going swimming if I don't have to do any diving or anything."

Michelle was pulling Daniel's socks on.

"You're not going, are you?" said Lisa.

"We can't stay," said Michelle. "We've still got a lot of work to do. We've only done a third of today's walking so far."

"Can he walk?" asked Poppy.

"He can walk underneath ladders," said Dawn. "They have ladders at their house, going all through the rooms, and he holds on to the rungs and walks along beautifully. You're really good at it, aren't you, Daniel?"

"Can I just show you something before you go?" asked Lisa. "Watch me."

She climbed up at the side of the weir and walked along the plank bridge where Michelle had been.

"We've seen that before," said Dawn. "Anyone can do that."

"No, wait," said Lisa. "Oh! Help!"

With a big grin on her face, she slipped through the rails at the side of the bridge, and let herself down into the water. Before Dawn could shout at her, Lisa was sliding down the weir, and a shower of water was fountaining up on either side of her. For a moment she disappeared under the water, but it was only a second before her head and shoulders popped up again, and Dawn could see that she was standing on the bottom.

"Oh, dear," laughed Lisa. "My foot slipped!" She waded to the side and climbed out.

"I wonder why it was so slippery?" said Poppy, and ran along the bridge to the place where Lisa had plunged into the water.

"I'm not going to watch this," said Dawn. "Jeff would kill me for letting them do it. Even Poppy is only supposed to do it when she's with Diane."

Poppy slid down the weir, and Lisa followed her.

"It is terribly slippery just there," said Lisa. "It's funny how slippery it is. I must try not to slip again." And she and Poppy slid, and climbed out, and slid again until Michelle and Daniel and Dawn were out of sight.

"There's no need for you to come swimming tomorrow if you don't feel like it," said Michelle as they left the park.

"No, I'll come," said Dawn. "I don't mind the pool so long as I don't have to feel ashamed of not really swimming."

Then she remembered that after the last swimming lesson she had left her swimming costume and towel in a damp bundle in a plastic bag, thinking that she would never need them again. They would be disgusting by now. And she remembered the sewn-up shoulder-straps.

"My swimming costume isn't very smart," she said.

"You'll be good company for Daniel, then," said Michelle, "in his underpants."

"You can't go for a picnic because you are going swimming?" said Jeff the next morning. "You are a strange girl. I thought you didn't like swimming."

"Michelle asked us all to go and help," said Lisa. "But then we remembered that Poppy's mother was going to take the day off specially. We couldn't hurt her feelings and not go, could we? And if Poppy and I aren't helping, Michelle will need Dawn to help with Daniel."

Poppy arrived early to pick Lisa up. "Bring your swimming things," she said. "Mummy says we're not going anywhere that we can swim, but you never know. We might just come across another weir or something, and it would be a shame not to have our things."

"You haven't been swimming in that weir, have you," asked Jeff, "after I asked you not to?"

"Not one stroke," said Lisa, which was true.

They left for their picnic, and Dawn set off for the swimming pool.

Michelle was in the changing room when she arrived, undressing Daniel. Daniel shouted in excitement when he saw Dawn, and waved his arms so violently that he hit his mother on the head.

"Hello there," said Michelle, rubbing her head. "You'd better get changed quickly. Once Daniel's ready he's not going to wait for anyone."

Dawn had rinsed out her swimming costume the night before, but it was still damp and difficult to put on. She pulled up the clammy straps. "You have to lock your clothes up," she told Michelle. "They took our clothes away once, because we had left them out on the benches."

"Oh, it's all changed since I was here last," said Michelle. "How do you work these locks? Ten pence, is it? My money keeps falling out of the slot."

Dawn sorted out the lockers and pinned the keys to her swimming costume. They went through to the pool.

"You have to wash your feet in the foot-bath first, Danny," Dawn told him.

Daniel looked around the huge noisy hall, and Dawn remembered how she had felt the first time she had come. It was a strange place, and must be even stranger for a little boy who spent most of his time in his quiet home, crawling from end to end of the house.

"It's all right," said Dawn. "I know it's noisy, but you'll get used to it. And it smells funny, too, doesn't it? But that's only to make sure there's no germs in the water. The smell won't do you any harm."

"You're right," said Michelle, "there is a smell. I hadn't noticed until you said so."

"Come and feel the water," said Dawn. "It's quite

warm. And look, at this end, it's shallow. You can sit in it."

Dawn watched as Michelle found arm-bands for Daniel. She threaded his thin arms through them, and then put him down in the shallow end of the pool, sitting on the highest step where the water only covered his legs. His face turned red and his mouth opened.

"It's all right," said Dawn quickly. She sat down next to him and put her arm round him. "It's only like a big bath. Here, sit on my lap."

Daniel changed his mind at the last minute and managed not to scream. He held on to Dawn with both hands and looked anxiously and intently into her face.

"He's never been in a bath," said Michelle. "We only have a shower at home. I shouldn't have just put him down like that. I can't think why I did. I should have known he would be terrified."

"You're not terrified now, are you, Dan?" said Dawn. "You don't need to be. I was scared the first time I came swimming, but I learnt to jump in last week, and I'm not scared of the water at all now." It was almost true. Daniel clung to Dawn's arms.

"Let's take him in a bit deeper," said Michelle. "There's not much point just sitting on the step there."

"No," said Dawn. "There's lot of things to get used to here. It's not just the water. Wait till he wants to get in deeper."

Dawn knew that she was right. Nobody should be made to get into deep water unless they wanted to. She found it was nice to sit in the warm shallow water, letting her feet float around. As she was looking after a small child, nobody could think it strange that such a large person as her was staying at the shallow end.

Michelle did not agree, but she did not argue about it. She waited impatiently for a few minutes, and then she went for a quick swim up and down the pool.

"I think I'll go in the deep pool for a couple of minutes," she said, "if you two are just going to sit there. It's ages since I had a good swim. Is that all right? I won't be long."

Dawn felt panic for a moment. She was in charge of this delicate little boy in this dangerous pool. Supposing he fell under the water, and she couldn't save him? But then, how could he fall? The water was shallow, and he was safely on her lap. While Dawn was reassuring herself, Daniel took his chance to smash his hand down into the water. They were both drenched. He was startled for a second, and then laughed at the top of his voice. When Michelle came back, they were half-way down the pool. Daniel was still clinging on to Dawn, but he was singing and splashing.

"That was fantastic," said Michelle. "I wouldn't want to change anything about my life, but there are just a few things that I do miss. One of them is having spare time to come for a good fast swim."

"Don't you have any free time at all?" asked Dawn.

"It's all free time," said Michelle. "I choose to spend it on Daniel. Don't worry about me. I'll enjoy it all the more when Dan can come and swim alongside me." She looked at Daniel, kicking up fountains with his feet. "You've got used to it now, have you?" she asked. "Let's see if you can float on your own now, Danny. The arm-bands will keep you up."

"I don't think he wants to yet," said Dawn. "Give him a chance. We've only been in the deep water a few minutes. And he still isn't quite sure whether he likes getting water in his eyes."

It was no longer cheating to keep her feet on the bottom. She needed to be standing firmly, to support Daniel in the water. It was tiring, keeping her legs bent the whole time, but it was lovely to see Daniel gradually becoming braver, clinging on a little less tightly, and sometimes letting his legs trail out behind him.

Michelle watched for a while. "You're right," she said. "I'm so used to organising everything for Daniel, and pushing him to take another step forward. I know I'm right about that, because he wouldn't have got anywhere without it, but I think you're right about this. There's no point in forcing him when it's all so strange to him. You do it your way."

163

They floated happily around the little pool. Other children with their bright red arm-bands bobbed by. No-one would have guessed that Daniel was different from them, or that when they climbed out of the pool and ran back into the changing room, he would have to be carried.

"It's nice that everyone's at the same level here," said Dawn. "Just heads bobbing about on the water."

"I think we'd better bob our way out," said Michelle. "Danny's starting to look cold. Look, his lips are going purple."

Daniel protested, but they lifted him out and wrapped him in a towel, and he enjoyed being bundled up and carried like a parcel back to the changing room. They dressed him together, one at each end, as quickly as they could, and then he sat on the bench, leaning back contentedly against the wall.

"Good swim, Dan?" Michelle asked. "Shall we come again?"

Daniel grinned and nodded.

"I could manage on my own," said Michelle, "now I know how everything works. But I would never have dared come on my own the first time. I wouldn't even have known how to work the lockers."

Dawn was dressed first. "I'll take him for a crawl in the passage outside," she said. "That will warm him up. Come on, Danny, come for a crawl." She carried him out of the changing room because the floor was wet. "Ready?" she said, and put him on the floor of the pasage. It was an ideal place for crawling, with a long smooth floor. Daniel roared gently. Something was wrong.

"What is it?" asked Dawn.

Daniel sat back on his heels and held his hands out to Dawn. She thought he wanted to be picked up again. "No, Dan, you must crawl, or you'll never learn to walk. Look, I'll go ahead of you. And up at the other end there's a drinks machine. I'll get you some Coke if Michelle says you're allowed it. Come on."

But Daniel would not move. He twisted his shoulders and reached out to Dawn so pitifully that she went to him and put her hands under his arms, ready to pick him up. But instead of bending his legs to lift them off the ground, Daniel pushed up against the floor.

"Do you want to walk, then?" Dawn asked. "All right, hold on to my hands."

She stood behind him with her hands high above his head, so that he would be in the same position as when he was walking along the ladders at home, but Daniel pulled his hands down. He took a step forward, still holding on to Dawn's hands. Then he let go of her completely and took another step, and another. Then he looked round to see that she was watching, lost his balance, and fell. Dawn just managed to catch him in time.

"You did it!" she screamed. "You did it! You walked on your own!"

Daniel leant against her, looking up with the widest smile on his face she had ever seen.

As he leant there, Michelle came out of the changing room carrying her bag of wet swimming things.

"Stop there!" called Dawn. "Just watch!" She turned Daniel round to face his mother, and whispered, "Go on, walk to your mum."

Daniel spread out his hands for balance, and took the five steps that brought him to Michelle. Michelle dropped her bag and caught him in her arms.

They did not need to tell Daniel that he was wonderful. He knew it, and they carried him home on their shoulders while he shouted to passers-by about his new achievement.

"I think the next thing we need to concentrate on is his speech," said Michelle. "It isn't really coming on as fast as I would like."

"You're never satisfied, are you?" said Dawn. "He's only learnt to walk on his own ten minutes ago, and now you're planning harder things for him to do."

"I'm not dissatisfied," said Michelle. "But I told you, I want him playing football and singing before we allow ourselves to sit back and relax."

"He might not be interested in football, you know," said Dawn, remembering how her father had expected her to enjoy swimming. "Not everyone likes the same things. He may turn out to be something quite different, like an archaeologist or a xylophone-player."

"Yes, you're right," said Michelle. "I'm not really making plans. All I want is for him to enjoy whatever he does choose to do."

"Well," said Dawn. "Whatever it is, I'll come and cheer him on next time we stay in Oxford. Dad said we can come again at half-term. You'll be scoring goals by then, won't you, Danny? Or sticking Greek urns together, or singing in concerts."

Daniel bounced on Michelle's shoulders and waved his arms in the air.

"You know you wanted to show Daniel some waterfalls?" said Dawn.

"Yes?" said Michelle. "We went to see the weir, didn't we?"

"Well, do you think we could go and see this other waterfall that I know?" said Dawn. "Tomorrow, so that Lisa can come as well? It wouldn't really be very educational for Daniel, but I think he would like it. It's in a restaurant in the centre of town, a place where they sell pizzas. I'd like Lisa to see him walking, and there won't be time for us to come to your house tomorrow. But it was her idea to come and help you, and I've had such a lovely time with you. It could be a sort of goodbye treat, because we have to go home in the afternoon. I've got nearly all my holiday money still left."

"You haven't had much time to spend it, have you?" said Michelle. "It's been hard work for you.

I'm afraid I've rather made use of you, because of so many of my usual helpers being away at the moment. And you've missed picnics and things because of us."

"I don't care about picnics," said Dawn. "You can have picnics any time. I've never seen someone take their very first steps before. I wouldn't have missed it for anything."

"Ask your friend Sarah to come, too," suggested Michelle. "To thank her for lending the toys. And you must get your Dad to come. We've got to show him that we haven't been wasting your time."

"And Poppy?" asked Dawn.

"And Poppy, of course," said Michelle. "And I'm paying. Pizza all round. Daniel and I haven't been out for a meal for a long time, have we, Dan?"

They had an early lunch, before the queues could gather on the winding green staircase at the pizza restaurant. Jeff carried the suitcase which had been Dawn and Lisa's wardrobe for two weeks. Lisa and Poppy ran down the stairs and chose two tables next to the waterfall. Jeff put the suitcase under the stairs.

"I know the plants are plastic," said Lisa, "but they are beautiful, aren't they, Daddy?"

Jeff looked at them thoughtfully. "The feathery ones are quite nice," he said. "The ferns. Not at all realistic, of course, but I suppose they have the advantage of not having spiders and bugs in them like real ones."

"What do you think, Dan?" Dawn asked. "Plants on the ceiling, and waterfalls on the floor! It's a nice place, isn't it?"

"It's very, very green," said Poppy. "I've never been anywhere quite so green. Even the tables and chairs."

"I'm glad I wore this dress," said Sarah, who was wearing a rainbow-coloured dress and a purple scarf round her neck. "Otherwise I might have got lost in the undergrowth." She began to fold a paper napkin into a boat shape.

"I can make a pecking bird out of paper," said Poppy, seizing another napkin. "These things are a bit floppy for folding, though."

Dawn folded a hat for Daniel. He wore it like a crown. He knew that Dawn and Lisa were going away today, but he felt that this was not a goodbye party so much as a celebration of the few steps that he had taken yesterday, and the few more he had taken today.

Sarah aimed a floppy paper aeroplane at Lisa. It looped feebly and fell into Michelle's lap.

Michelle picked it up. "I've been meaning to thank you," she said, "for lending us all those lovely wind-up toys. They've been very useful. Danny loves them. But I'm afraid they aren't all in quite such good shape as they were when we borrowed them."

"That's all right," said Sarah. "I'm glad that someone has found a use for them. I can't resist buying clockwork toys when I find them in shops, but it's terrible just to take them home and put them on my shelves and never let them be played with. I didn't lend you my oldest ones. I've got a tin engine that my mother had when she was little, but I thought that might be too fragile. Did Dawn's idea work, of having them go along ahead of Daniel, to lure him on?"

"Sort of," said Michelle. "Would you like to come round afterwards and see them in action?"

Dawn listened and felt pleased. Perhaps Sarah would start helping Michelle. Dawn thought that she was the sort of person who would be good at persuading Daniel to crawl for miles, and who would be properly delighted by every step he took.

"Maybe there's time now for you to explain a little about the method you are following with Daniel?" Jeff asked Michelle. "Dawn has told me a bit about it, and it doesn't sound quite as crazy as it seemed when I came into your house last week and found you spinning Daniel round in circles. I would really like to know more about it."

Dawn cut up Daniel's pizza and she and Lisa took turns to help him spike pieces on his fork and get them somewhere near his mouth. He insisted on putting three straws in everyone's drinks. They all had to celebrate today.

"What pizza did you order?" asked Sarah, peering at the other plates. "I think they've given me the cardboard and wood shavings sort by mistake."

"They're meant to taste like that," said Lisa. "It's lovely, isn't it? No bones, or pips, just pure food. All you have to do is chew it."

The fountain sprinkled green and orange drops beside them. Daniel saw his second waterfall, and had to be prevented from diving into it. Sarah sailed paper boats in the pool until they went soggy and had to be dredged out and put in the ash-tray. Poppy and Lisa told jokes. Poppy knew even worse ones than Lisa.

"That was a real party," said Michelle, as they climbed the stairs after the meal. By now a long queue had formed of people waiting to eat, and Jeff, carrying Daniel as well as the suitcase, had to push his way up the stairs. "We don't get to many parties. Thank you very much for joining us."

"It's not long before your coach leaves," Jeff told Dawn and Lisa. "We'd better say goodbye to everyone."

Michelle set off home with Daniel, who still had most of the day's crawling to do. Sarah went with them. Poppy said goodbye and went to her busstop.

Jeff took Dawn and Lisa to the coach station. He put their suitcase in the boot, and told the driver where they were to get off. They knelt up on the back seat to wave goodbye.

"I don't want to start waving too soon," said Lisa. "Otherwise you can carry on for hours, and you feel silly. Let's wait till the bus is just about moving away."

The driver had started his engine, but the front doors were still open. Jeff stood on the pavement looking uncomfortable.

"He's trying to time it just right as well. I wish you could talk through these windows."

"What's the time!" she shouted.

Jeff touched his ear and looked puzzled.

Lisa screamed it again, and pointed to her wrist. Jeff nodded.

172

"He didn't know what I was saying," she said.

"Look, he's going," said Dawn. Jeff was disappearing through a crowd by a different bus-stop. "He didn't say goodbye at all."

Lisa looked at Dawn, waiting to be told that Jeff had not really gone.

"Perhaps he was so upset to see us go that he couldn't bear to wait any longer," said Dawn. It did not sound likely, but it pleased Lisa. But suddenly there was a scuffle at the front of the coach and Jeff came running down the gangway.

"Hurry up!" shouted the driver, revving up his engine. "I'm leaving five minutes ago!"

Jeff pushed something into Dawn's lap. "I must go," he said. "Have a good journey! 'Bye!" He kissed each of them quickly on the top of the head, and ran back along the gangway. The driver closed the doors and the coach began to move away from the pavement. Jeff stood on the pavement waving.

"'Bye, Daddy!" screamed Lisa.

"'Bye, Dad!" shouted Dawn.

They waved until he was out of sight.

"You called him Dad," said Lisa.

"Did I?" said Dawn. They looked at what Jeff had put on Dawn's lap. It was a pile of comics.

"So many comics!" said Lisa. "Look, *Penny the Pesky Pest*! And *Sally-Jo*! Mum loves *Sally-Jo*. She told me she used to get it when she was little."

They looked through the heap of comics. They had never seen so many at one time, except at the dentist's, but these were brand new and crisp, and three of them had free gifts inside, a plastic bracelet, a badge and a toffee bar, which you never get at the dentist.

"I thought he didn't like comics?" said Lisa.

"He doesn't," said Dawn. "But I suppose he thinks it's all right for us to like whatever we like, even if it isn't what he likes."

She snapped the toffee bar in two and they chewed a piece each as the coach sped along the motorway to where Mum would be waiting for them.

MORE WALKER PAPERBACKS
For You to Enjoy

☐	0-7445-1475-4	*Rook* by Gabriel Alington	£2.99
☐	0-7445-1431-2	*In Between Times* by Hannah Cole	£2.99
☐	0-7445-1448-7	*The Worm Charmers* by Nicholas Fisk	£2.99
☐	0-7445-1420-7	*Pig in the Middle* by Sam Llewellyn	£2.99
☐	0-7445-1464-9	*Antar and the Eagles* by William Mayne	£2.99
☐	0-7445-1332-4	*Worlds Apart* by Jill Murphy	£2.99
☐	0-7445-1447-9	*The Time Tree* by Enid Richemont	£2.99
☐	0-7445-1465-7	*Freddie and the Enormouse* by Hugh Scott	£2.99

**Walker Paperbacks are available from most booksellers. They are also available
by post: just tick the titles you want, fill in the form below and send it to
Walker Books Ltd, PO Box 11, Falmouth, Cornwall TR10 9EN.**

Please send a cheque or postal order and allow the following for postage and packing:
UK, BFPO and Eire – 50p for first book, plus 10p for
each additional book to a maximum charge of £2.00.
Overseas Customers – £1.25 for first book,
plus 25p per copy for each additional book.
Prices are correct at time of going to press, but are subject to change without notice.

Name —————————————————————————

Address ————————————————————————

—————————————————————————————

—————————————————————————————